"Tucker, put r
he scooped her
and all.

"No."

"This is ridiculous. I'm perfectly capable of—"

"Alison." Her name was a rumble of sensuous sound, a puff of warm air against her cheek. She felt invisible strings pulling her toward him. She slowly turned and looked into sky blue eyes, and a soft moan escaped her lips. Then she gazed at his lips, and her heart raced at the thought of those lips moving on hers.

"Tucker—"

"Shh."

He kissed her.

As soon as Tucker's mouth melted over Alison's, he knew he was powerless to stop. The taste, the scent, the feel of Alison in his arms was robbing him of reason, filling him with want. Kissing her was—heaven. . . .

WHAT ARE *LOVESWEPT* ROMANCES?

They are stories of true romance and touching emotion. We believe those two very important ingredients are constants in our highly sensual and very believable stories in the *LOVESWEPT* line. Our goal is to give you, the reader, stories of consistently high quality that may sometimes make you laugh, sometimes make you cry, but are always fresh and creative and contain many delightful surprises within their pages.

Most romance fans read an enormous number of books. Those they truly love, they keep. Others may be traded with friends and soon forgotten. We hope that each *LOVESWEPT* romance will be a treasure—a "keeper." We will always try to publish

LOVE STORIES YOU'LL NEVER FORGET
BY AUTHORS YOU'LL ALWAYS REMEMBER

The Editors

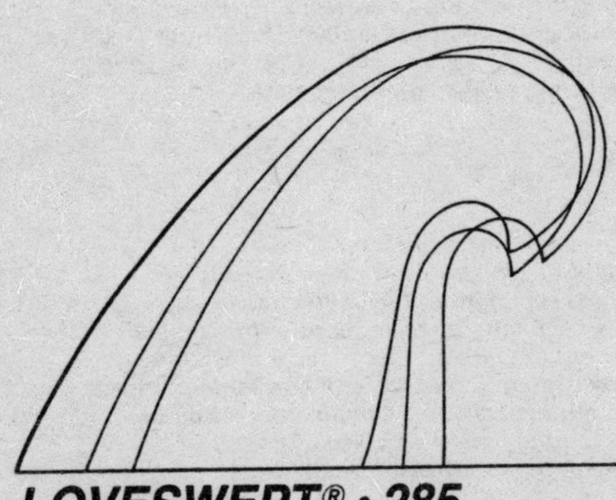

LOVESWEPT® • 285

Joan Elliott Pickart

Tucker Boone

BANTAM BOOKS
TORONTO • NEW YORK • LONDON • SYDNEY • AUCKLAND

TUCKER BOONE

A Bantam Book / October 1988

ISBN 0-553-21938-3

Published simultaneously in the United States and Canada

Bantam Books are published by Bantam Books, a division of Bantam Doubleday Dell Publishing Group, Inc. Its trademark, consisting of the words "Bantam Books" and the portrayal of a rooster, is Registered in U.S. Patent and Trademark Office and in other countries. Marca Registrada. Bantam Books, 666 Fifth Avenue, New York, New York 10103.

PRINTED IN THE UNITED STATES OF AMERICA

O 0 9 8 7 6 5 4 3 2 1

One

Alison Murdock flung the pen onto the top of the desk, then watched in amazement as it bounced up, flipped in the air, and landed with a splash in her coffee mug.

"Olympic form," a deep voice said. "I give that dive an eight-point-five."

"Cute," Alison said. She shot a quick glare at the handsome man standing in front of her desk, then looked at the pen again. "I couldn't do that again if I tried. That remarkable accident, however, doesn't seem quite as remarkable as it might, given what a lousy day I've had. Blak."

"Blak? Shall I quote you on that?"

"Don't do anything to make me laugh," Alison said, leaning back in her chair, "because I'm in a crummy mood, and I intend to stay in a crummy mood. I've had it, Nick. I swear to heaven, this is the last straw. So what if I'm one of the junior members of this law firm? Why do I get stuck with all the garbage cases?"

"Well, you—"

"No, don't say it." Alison got to her feet. "Don't say I have to be patient."

Nick raised his hands in a gesture of peace. "I wouldn't dream of it. The word *patient* will never again cross my luscious Italian lips. Let it not be said that Nick Capoletti told Alison Murdock to be patient. There. How's that?"

Alison laughed, "Darn you, I'm trying to stay angry."

"Anger burns up energy that could be put to better use as passion."

"Says you."

"Knows me," he said, wiggling his eyebrows at her. "Why are you so ticked off today in particular?"

She picked up a file and waved it. "This new case I was given. A custody battle in a divorce."

"Challenging."

"Stupid. They're fighting for custody of the tulip bulbs. They had them shipped in from Holland, and they both want them. I've got *Mrs.* Tulip."

"Stupid," Nick said, nodding.

"And you, Lucky Capoletti, as my assigned secretary and paralegal, get to go to the law library to see if there are any cases similar to this to set precedent."

"Hey! How come you get all the garbage cases around here?" Nick said, then laughed and sank onto a chair.

"Oh, stop," Alison said, glaring at him again. She picked up another file. "Here's a beaut. I can't find my client. I've never met the man, his phone is disconnected, we've written him three letters asking him to contact me immediately regarding an important matter, and nothing. I've had it with this jerk. I'm going to drive out to the address given here and see him in person."

"Good idea," Nick said. "We're running out of time on that one."

"I know." She sat down again and flipped open the file. "Tap into your data-bank brain and tell me where this street is."

"I typed the letters, remember? They were headed to one of those mini ranches on the outside of town, those fifteen-acre numbers in that section that was fought over years ago. Some megabucks boys wanted to rezone for condos: others wanted a game reserve. It ended in compromise and was split up into a dozen mini ranches."

Alison sighed. "I wish I had a photographic memory like you."

"I love it. I can remember every woman I've ever . . . uh, forget that."

"You could be a brilliant attorney, Nick."

He shrugged. "Maybe one of these days. I like what I'm doing now."

"Researching tulips?" Alison nearly shrieked.

"Sure. Hey, I'm only thirty. I have plenty of time to decide my future. I, madam, have patience, which is not one of your virtues."

"No, it is not," Alison said, getting to her feet again. "I'm twenty-eight, and I have no intention of spending years as one of the junior members of this outfit, being given these idiotic cases. Okay, it's"—she glanced at her watch—"four-fifteen. I'm going out to this yo-yo's house and sit there until he comes home from work. Providing, of course, that he works."

"Okay, boss," Nick said. "Give him hell. We really are running out of time on that deal."

"Precisely. All right, Mr."—she looked at the name on the tab of the file—"Mr. Tucker Boone, I'm on my way."

The Houston traffic was heavy; horns blared and bumpers fulfilled the potential of their name as July and high humidity caused tempers to flare. Alison drove her five-year-old compact car at a crawl, wishing for the umpteenth time that it was air-conditioned. She'd shed her gray suit jacket the moment she'd left the law offices of Brinker, Brinker, and Abbot, and her pale pink blouse was sticking to her back. She could feel the perspiration trickling between her full breasts, and called Mr. Tucker Boone an unladylike name.

"You're a pain in the patookus, Boone," she muttered. "You could pay attention to your mail, you know. Your phone is probably disconnected because you didn't pay the bill, or you just didn't check the mail to find the bill to pay. Brother. Why me?" She cautioned herself then to stop talking and focused on her driving.

At last the traffic thinned as Alison followed the directions Nick had given her. She passed an impressive-looking house with a red barn in the distance and realized she'd reached the area of the mini ranches.

Snazzy, she thought, driving past the second one.

There was definitely class and money out here. Maybe this deal with Tucker Boone was going to be just fine, after all.

A few minutes later Alison's heart sank as she saw the number on the mailbox she was approaching. She slowed, her horrified gaze sweeping over the large two-story house set well back from the road. It was nearly devoid of paint, the front steps were sagging, and weeds grew in abundance among the tall trees. There was a barn in the distance, also in need of paint, and two sets of corrals were missing more slats of wood than were in place.

"Wonderful," Alison said, turning into the driveway.

The road was deeply rutted, and Alison was jarred and jiggled until she came to the end of the drive. She turned off the ignition, grabbed her briefcase, and got out of the car. She would not, she decided, put on her jacket and swelter even more for Tucker Boone.

Alison made her way carefully across the yard, virtually tiptoeing to avoid snagging her panty hose and to keep her two-inch heels from sinking into the dirt. Her gaze was riveted on the ground, covered by knee-high weeds. This patch was a perfect little Garden of Eden, of which Texas had far too many in Alison's opinion. She looked up just in time to keep from bumping into a tree.

A tall tree. A tall tree with lots of leaves that created an umbrella of shade. A tree that had a matching one about ten feet beyond it. And suspended between the two was a hammock.

Alison slowly moved forward and stopped at the

side of the hammock. Her eyes widened, and her heart began to beat a tattoo.

"Dear Lord," she whispered.

There, in all his stretched-out-in-the-hammock glory, was, without a doubt, the most gorgeous man she had ever seen.

He was sleeping. Long, thick lashes fanned out on tanned skin. Rugged cheekbones. Gleaming shaggy blond-brown hair on a nicely shaped head. Oh-so kissable lips slightly parted. Clad only in faded cut-offs slung low on narrow hips, his body was bronzed and beautifully proportioned with muscles. His chest was a work of art; covered in tawny curls and glistening with a light sheen of perspiration from the heat. A smattering of white-blond hair graced his legs, and he even had attractive toes, long and gracefully arched. The man, who was maybe thirty-five, was incredibly handsome.

"Dear Lord," Alison whispered again. Was this Tucker Boone?

She'd have to wake him up and ask him, Alison decided. And she *would* . . . in a minute. But first she'd look him over, head to perfect toes, just one more time. After all, perfection should be appreciated, like a fine painting or a sculpture. Goodness, those cutoffs were snug and—

"Want to cop a feel?" a deep voice rumbled.

Alison yelped, splaying her hand over her heart and teetering slightly.

The long lashes lifted to reveal sky-blue eyes, then as Alison watched in rather dazed fascination, a smile began to take form on those unbelievable lips and widened, revealing teeth as straight and white as a row of Chiclets. Was this, Alison wondered again, Tucker Boone?

"Mr. Boone?" she asked tentatively, her voice a mere whisper. *Alison,* she thought, berating herself, *that was not professional.* She cleared her throat. "Mr. Boone, I presume?"

The man chuckled, and Alison instantly knew it was the sexiest sound she'd ever heard. A queer sensation slithered along her spine, and she cleared her throat again.

"Yep," the man said. "I'm Tucker Boone." He yawned. "Who are you?" Whoever she was, Tucker mused, she was nice to wake up to. She looked like a doll—small-boned, no more than five-three or four, her short, dark brown curls a cap around her head. She had big brown eyes, lush breasts pushing against her pink blouse, and just enough hips to be interesting. Nice legs too. Pretty face with delicate features. All around, a delectable package, whoever she was.

"I'm Alison Murdock, Mr. Boone. I'm an attorney, and I've been trying to get in touch with you. Your phone is disconnected and you haven't responded to my letters, so I came out here to see you."

Tucker frowned. "Am I being sued?"

"Not that I know of."

"That's comforting," he said, his lashes drifting down again.

"Mr. Boone, please don't go back to sleep. It's imperative that I speak with you."

He opened one eye. "Imperative?"

"Yes. We're running out of time."

He opened his other eye, and the grin slid back into place. "To do what, Counselor?"

Patience, Alison, she told herself. "Look, do you think we could get out of this heat? What I have to explain to you is rather complicated."

"Are you positive that I'm not being sued?"

"Mr. Boone, please."

"All right, all right. Let's go into the house."

Alison blinked and took a step backward as six feet of masculinity rolled out of the hammock in a smooth motion and stood towering above her. She caught a whiff of soap and sweat, deciding the combination was definitely appealing.

And the man himself? Alison asked herself. Well, Tucker Boone was beautiful, there was no denying that. And, yes, somewhere deep within her she was reacting to him on a purely female level, her body tingling and fluttering. But intellectually she knew he wasn't even close to being her type. He'd been snoozing away in his hammock, while his house and property were in shambles. And that, in Alison's view, was disgraceful. Great big strong Tucker Boone was lazy—a trait she couldn't tolerate. Now, if she could manage to stop gawking at his magnificent body like an adolescent, she could pull this meeting off quickly and professionally and be done with this man.

"After you, ma'am," Tucker said, sweeping his arm toward the house.

"Thank you, Mr. Boone," she said primly.

She started toward the house, only to discover immediately that she had to resort again to tiptoeing because of her high heels. The throaty chuckle from behind her caused her to grit her teeth and quicken her step, hoping that she didn't look like a mincing horse.

Tucker followed slowly behind Alison Murdock, unable to hide his smile. She was attempting, he knew, to come across as a highfalutin lawyer, all cool and businesslike, but at the moment that image was blown. The way she was walking caused her enticing little bottom to wiggle, and her hips to sashay just as nice as you please. And he'd seen her looking him over while she thought he was asleep. She hadn't missed one inch of him. Of course, he'd checked her out, too, and definitely liked what he had seen. Yes, indeed, Alison Murdock was a delectable package.

"Whoa," Tucker said as Alison got to the steps of the porch. "I don't trust those steps, even with a featherweight like you."

Alison stopped.

Tucker moved past her and bounded up onto the porch. He turned to look down at her where she stood staring at the three sagging steps.

"Nope. Guess not," he said. He jumped back down, moved behind her, planted his large hands on her waist, and lifted her up onto the porch.

"Lord!" Alison exclaimed. Tucker jumped back onto the porch. "You could have warned me you were going to do that," she said, glaring up at him. Heat. She could still feel the heat from where Tucker Boone's hands had held her. He was so strong. "You . . . you surprised me."

He shrugged. "Sorry. It got the job done." His hands had nearly spanned her tiny waist, Tucker mused. She was so small, so fragile, that she brought out protective instincts in a man, making him intensely aware of his own size and strength. When he took Alison into his arms, held her, kissed her, he'd have to be gentle, treat her like fine china, and . . . *Whoa, Boone,* he cautioned himself, immediately wondering where those thoughts were coming from. "Shall we go inside?"

Alison lifted her chin. "Certainly."

Tucker pulled on the screen door, which squeaked on its hinges, and stepped back for Alison to enter. She smelled good, he reflected as she passed him. She smelled fresh, womanly, like flowers.

Inside, Alison quickly glanced around. The living room was large, with a beamed ceiling and a huge stone fireplace. The walls were paneled in knotty pine, and chocolate-colored carpeting stretched in all directions. The decorating, she surmised, had been done with a rustic flair, which lost something in the layer of dust on the end tables and the white sheets covering most of the furniture. An oatmeal-colored sofa was visible, and Alison walked over to it and sat down, her briefcase balanced on her knees.

"Care for something to drink?" Tucker said. "Beer? Lemonade?"

"Lemonade would be nice," Alison said, silently tacking on a plea for him to put a shirt on. Her nervous system had had all of that enticing bare chest she could take for one day.

"One lemonade coming right up," Tucker said, striding across the room. "I wonder where I left my shirt."

Find it, Alison thought crossly. She placed the

briefcase on the cushion next to her and snapped it open, taking out the file with Tucker Boone's name on the tab. She blew a puff of air up over her face, hoping to fan her flushed cheeks.

It was no cooler in the house than it had been outside, she realized. And, darn it, she could still feel the heat of Tucker's hands where they'd held her around the waist. Suddenly it seemed urgent to conclude her business, go home, stand under the shower—and escape the disturbing presence of Mr. Tucker Boone.

Tucker returned and gave Alison a glass filled with lemonade and tinkling ice cubes. With a can of beer in his hand he sank into a leather chair by the fireplace, stretched out his long legs, and crossed them at the ankle.

He'd found a shirt, Alison noticed, taking a sip of her lemonade. A blue chambray, which he'd put on but failed to tuck in or button, so that half of his chest was still exposed. Why did he look just as sexy wearing an open shirt as he had with no shirt at all?

Tucker took a deep swallow of beer, and Alison watched in fascination as Tucker's Adam's apple moved in the strong column of his tanned throat.

Wonderful, she thought dryly. Now she was getting all charged up over the man's neck! She really had to get out of the heat—and away from Tucker Boone.

She set her glass on a dusty end table. "Mr. Boone—"

"Tucker. Call me Tucker. This is Texas, you know,

darlin'. Everyone is friendly here. You call me Tucker and I'll call you Alison." He smiled at her.

Alison's heart skipped a beat. "Fine. Now, then, Tucker, let's get down to business, shall we?"

The smile grew bigger. "You bet."

Damn, Alison thought frantically, that smile was lethal. And those blue, blue eyes of his were . . . And his face, his body, his voice, his . . . Alison blinked hard and got a grip on her runaway thoughts.

"Mr. Boone, I work for Brinker, Brinker, and Abbot, attorneys-at-law. Mr. Brinker handled the affairs of your late grandfather"—she flipped open the file and glanced at it—"Mr. Jeremy Daniel Boone, who—"

"Which one?" Tucker asked, interrupting.

"Which one who?" Alison said, frowning. "Did you have more than one grandfather named Jeremy Daniel Boone?"

"No, I mean, which Brinker? Old Brinker or young Brinker?"

"They're both as old as the hills."

Tucker hooted.

"What I mean is," Alison said quickly, "is that the senior Mr. Brinker was your grandfather's attorney. I understand that they were friends for many years. Your grandfather's will was on file with our firm, despite the fact that Jeremy Daniel Boone had lived in England since the end of World War II."

"Yep, he liked it over there," Tucker said, then took another swallow of beer.

"That's nice. Anyway, upon his death two months ago, his will was executed in the proper manner. I have no idea what that document contained."

"A whole slew of stuff, including my inheritance of this place," Tucker said, glancing around. "I didn't even know that Jeremy owned it. I came here and hadn't done more than get the utilities turned on when I was called away again on an emergency. I just got back last night."

"Oh, I see. Well, your phone is disconnected."

Tucker shrugged. "Somebody screwed up. There's a stack of mail around here someplace, but I haven't had a chance to look at it. I was wiped out after flying in from South America. Jet lag is not fun."

Poor baby, Alison thought sympathetically, then felt a twinge of guilt. And she'd judged Tucker lazy when he really was suffering from jet lag. Shame on her for jumping to conclusions, something an attorney should never do.

"Well, that explains the general . . . disarray of this place," she said, smiling brightly.

"Disarray? I don't know," Tucker said. "It has a sort of earthy charm the way it is."

Alison frowned. Reinstate lazy, she thought. Or add weird. Earthy charm? The house and grounds were a disaster.

"Anyway," she went on, "Mr. Brinker has received an addendum to your grandfather's will that was forwarded from an attorney in England. That addendum was given to me to process."

Tucker drained the beer can and tossed it onto the grate in the fireplace, where it landed with a clang. "Yeah?"

Alison stared at the beer can for a long moment, then redirected her gaze to Tucker. "Yes, that's why I'm here. While Jeremy Daniel Boone's bequest to you in the addendum to the original will is rather unusual, it's perfectly legal and was agreed upon by the parties involved. Well, you probably didn't agree, as I doubt you know anything about it. Then again, maybe you do. Or—"

"Alison, you've lost me."

"Oh. Sorry. You see, Tucker, your grandfather left you his gentleman's gentleman."

Tucker straightened in his chair. "His what?"

"In short, you've inherited a butler."

Tucker rose to his feet. "A butler?"

Alison blinked. "I know it's unusual. I mean, we're talking about a living, breathing human being here. But this Mr."—she looked at the file again—"Mr. Mercer Martin was your grandfather's gentleman's gentleman for thirty years. Mr. Martin has no family, nowhere to go. Jeremy Daniel Boone wanted his loyal butler to have a home, Mr. Martin agreed, and all the legal formalities were attended to. Mr. Mercer Martin arrives in Houston in two days to take up his post with you."

Tucker planted his large hands on his narrow hips. "That's nuts."

"It's perfectly legal. According to the document I was given, Mr. Martin does more than just answer the door like a run-of-the-mill butler. He's an old-fashioned gentleman's gentleman. He cooks, sees to your wardrobe, tends to your social calendar, all kinds of terrific stuff. Gentleman's gentlemen sound like very handy fellows to have around." She paused. "That is, apparently he's very efficient."

"This is crazy," Tucker roared. Alison jumped. "I visited my grandfather a few times in that drafty old castle of his in England. There was a tall, skinny guy sneaking around, carrying trays of little sandwiches with no crusts. He poured tea from a silver pot. He never said a word, just poured tea and plunked down trays of sandwiches with no crusts. And now you're saying that creepy guy belongs to me? Well, guess what, lady? I don't want him!"

"Mr. Boone . . . Tucker . . . I realize this is a bit of a shock and that one would think that a living person couldn't be inherited. But I assure you that it's all very legal, due to the careful wording of the documents by the attorneys in charge. Your grandfather was concerned about the future of Mr. Martin. He, your grandfather, chose you over everyone else he might have considered, to make a home for Mr. Martin. Plus, you get the benefit of Mr. Martin's expert services."

Tucker crossed his arms over his broad chest and cocked a tawny eyebrow at Alison. She smiled at him pleasantly.

"There's just one little problem here, Alison darlin', Tucker said tightly.

"Oh?"

"I am not a gentleman!" he said, thumping himself on the chest.

That wasn't funny, Alison told herself quickly and firmly. Despite the fact that the yuppie types she dated knocked themselves out proving their oh so gentlemanly behavior to enhance their image, and that here stood a half-dressed man emphatically declaring that he wasn't a gentleman, it was *not* funny.

Oh, Lord, she thought in the next instant. Yes, it was. It was hysterically funny.

Alison tried. She really did. She pursed her lips so tightly together that her cheeks puffed out and her eyes nearly crossed. But when she looked up again at the stormy expression on Tucker Boone's face as he towered over her, it was just too much.

She laughed until she could hardly breathe and tears of merriment spilled onto her cheeks. She wrapped her arms around her stomach, leaned her head back on the top of the sofa, and laughed until she was close to getting a case of the hiccups.

Tucker's eyes widened as he stared at her. She was flipping out, he thought incredulously. Alison Murdock was laughing herself silly. But what a fantastic sound. Her laughter was real, honest, dancing through the air, bouncing off the walls, and landing with a thud of heat low in his belly. It was beautiful. Alison was beautiful.

However, he went on mentally, narrowing his eyes, he was not in the habit of standing quietly by while someone laughed at Tucker Boone!

"Knock it off!" he yelled.

Alison gasped. She popped up pencil-straight on the edge of the sofa, folded her hands in her lap, and drew in a huge gulp of air. "There. I'm fine . . . I hope." She looked up at Tucker. "I do apologize. That was very unprofessional of me. It's just that what you said was so . . . oh, geez, don't get me started again." One last giggle escaped from her lips.

"That's it," Tucker said through clenched teeth. "You think it's funny that I said that I'm not a gentleman, right? You attorneys like proof, right? Well, okay, Miss Alison Murdock, you asked for it."

"Well, I . . . oh!"

Tucker's large hands gripped Alison's upper arms and hauled her to her feet. In the next instant his mouth came down hard onto hers in a rough kiss, his tongue parting her lips and plummeting into her mouth.

Alison's eyes were wide with shock, and she splayed her hands flat on Tucker's chest to push him away. Her fingers were half on his shirt, and half on moist, curly hair and warm skin over ropy muscles. Trying to move Tucker Boone was like attempting to shove away a huge, solid tree, and Alison gave up the effort.

Her senses, she realized, were suddenly on red alert. Tucker tasted like beer and peppermint. He smelled of soap and fresh air and sweat. And the kiss was gentle, no longer punishing. Changing to soft and sensuous, his kiss was igniting a fire storm in her body. She felt Tucker's heart thudding wildly beneath her hands, hands that were creeping up to encircle his neck. She heard the groan rumble from his chest as his arms moved to her back, bringing her even closer to his heated body.

Tucker knew he was in trouble, knew the exact moment when the kiss changed from one prompted by irritation to one spurred by pure passion. He nestled Alison to him, fitting her tiny form against his rugged contours. She felt as fragile as he'd known she would, and he held her carefully, as though she were a delicate butterfly. Her lips were soft, her mouth a sweet haven, her aroma crowding his senses. His body tightened as images flitted through his mind of sharing more, much more, than just a kiss with Alison Murdock.

He wanted all of her.

With a driving need like none he'd experienced before, he wanted to make love with this woman, a woman who was now returning his kiss in total abandon, meeting his tongue, pressing her full breasts against his chest.

Ohh, yes, he thought, he was most definitely in trouble. He had to end this kiss . . . right now.

Tucker tore his mouth from Alison's and drew a raspy breath as he gently pulled her arms from his neck. He looked at her closed eyes, the long lashes resting on flushed skin, at her moist, kiss-swollen lips. He stifled a groan, along with the burning urge to claim her mouth once again, and released her arms. As Alison slowly opened her eyes he took a step back.

"That"—he cleared his throat—"should prove my point, Miss Murdock."

"Hmm? Prove your what?"

"Dammit!" Tucker thundered, frustration causing him to react angrily.

Alison jumped and snapped out of her semi-trance. "Oh! Oh, my goodness."

"Do you have it yet?" he asked gruffly. "I'm not a gentleman!"

Alison put her hand over her heart, relieved to find that it was returning to a normal rhythm. "You may not be a gentleman," she said breathlessly, "but you're a wingdinger of a kisser!" Dear Lord, she thought, how mortifying to have blurted those words. She gulped with embarrassment. She'd been carried away by his kiss, desperately wanted another one, or two or . . .

Tucker stabbed one long finger in the air. "See? I don't qualify for a gentleman's gentleman. Get it? You'll have to make other arrangements for Mercer Martin and his sandwiches with no crusts."

"But I can't do that," Alison said. "Everything is in motion. Mr. Martin arrives in two days to take up residence with you."

"The hell he does!"

"Tucker, please, you don't understand. Mercer Martin has no family, nowhere to go. Your grandfather did this for Mercer as an act of kindness. You can't turn the man away."

"Watch me," Tucker said, dragging his hand through his thick hair. "I don't want him here."

"Why not? You said yourself that he's very quiet." She glanced around. "He could dust. Yes, dust, and help make this place a tad more . . . livable."

"No."

Alison pressed her hand to her forehead. "Now, listen," she said, dropping her hand, "let's compromise, okay? You let Mercer come here when he arrives, and in the meantime I'll speak with Mr. Brinker and inform him that other arrangements will have to be made."

Tucker ran his hand over the back of his neck. "I don't like it."

"It's only until we can find another position for Mercer. I'm sure it won't take long. There must be oodles of people eager to have a gentleman's gentleman. Okay? Please?"

Ah, damn, Tucker thought, looking at the expression on her beautiful face. How could a man say no to big, dark, pleading eyes like that? And how could a man forget those lips and the way they'd felt moving beneath his? Damn.

"A few days," he said. "He can stay a few days, that's it. Brinker had better get off his butt and find somewhere else for Mercer Martin to go."

"I'll tell Mr. Brinker to get off his . . . I mean, we'll tend to the matter posthaste." Alison paused and frowned. "I realize that you don't like sandwiches without crusts, Tucker, but you could tell Mercer not to cut the crusts off. I'd think you'd be glad to have some help around here. This is a very large house."

"I live alone, Alison," Tucker said. "I like it that way. I'm not even sure if I want to keep this place. I travel around a lot. Besides, if Mercer Martin moves in here, I'll be responsible for him. I just . . . just don't like the idea that another person's welfare is my responsibility. That's not my cup of tea. Tea . . . I hate tea. Mercer is big on serving tea. No, this isn't going to work out at all. Tell Brinker!"

"Yes. Yes, I will," Alison said. She picked up the file and put it in the briefcase. "I'll be in touch."

"What time do we go to the airport to pick up Mercer?"

Alison looked quickly at Tucker. "We?"

"Of course. Hell, I wouldn't even know what to say to the guy. Besides, you've got to explain to him that his staying here is only temporary."

"Me?"

"I'm not going to tell him. You legal eagles got me into this mess, and you can get me out. Mercer arrives in two days? Fine. I rented a car when I got in. Where do you want me to pick you up to go to the airport?"

"But . . ." Alison threw up her hands. "All right. I suppose I do have some responsibility here. Mercer's flight is early, ten something. You might as well pick me up at home." She took a pad and pen from her briefcase and wrote down her address. "Here," she said, handing him the paper. "Maybe I should drive out here instead, so you don't have to take me back into town later."

"No, I'll pick you up. I don't want any slipups that leave me having to tell Mercer the news once we get out here to the house."

"Whatever." Alison sighed, then paused. "I bet the tulip bulbs are going to be easier than this."

"The what?"

"Never mind." She snapped the briefcase closed. "I'll see you in two days, Tucker. I guess you should pick me up about eight-thirty because of the traffic." She started toward the door.

"Whoa," Tucker said, striding after her. "The front steps, remember? I can't have an attorney taking a header off my porch. I'd get my butt sued for sure."

"I'll jump."

"Not a chance." He scooped her up into his arms, briefcase and all.

"Darn it, Tucker, put me down." She stared straight ahead, refusing to look at him.

"No."

"This is ridiculous. I'm perfectly capable of—"

"Alison."

Her name was a rumble of sensuous sound, a puff

of warm air against her cheek. A tiny voice within her told Alison not to move her head and look at Tucker. A stronger message from somewhere deep within her demanded that she yield to the invisible strings pulling her toward him. She slowly turned her head to gaze into sky blue eyes that were so very close to her, to see lips that caused her heart to race at the thought of them moving on hers.

"Tucker, I . . ."

"Shh."

He kissed her.

As Tucker's mouth melted over Alison's he knew he hadn't planned to do this. He also admitted to himself that he was powerless to stop. The taste, the aroma, the feel of Alison in his arms was robbing him of all reason, filling him with want. He was drinking of her sweetness like a thirsty man, seeking more than he would be able to have. But, oh, Lord, Alison Murdock was heaven itself.

Alison leaned into Tucker's kiss, her hands tightly gripping her briefcase. She parted her lips, met his tongue, and drifted into a hazy place of desire. She was held tightly to him by strong arms against a rock-hard chest, suspended in pleasure, unaware of anything else but the wondrous sensations coursing through her.

This was just so wonderful, she thought dreamily. And just so . . . wrong.

Alison's eyes flew open, and she lifted her head with a jerky motion. Her gaze lingered for a moment on Tucker's half-closed eyes, seeing the smoky hue of desire in their blue depths.

"You shouldn't have done that," she said, her voice shaky.

"Sue me," he said, his own voice raspy. "But do note, Counselor, that you kissed me back. Equal billing."

Alison raised one hand and patted her hair in a nervous gesture as she stared at her briefcase.

"Yes, you're right," she said. "That was very unprofessional of me. Would you please put me down?"

"Nope." Tucker kicked open the screen door and strode out onto the porch with Alison still held tightly in his arms.

"This is absurd."

"Nope." He jumped off the porch and landed on the balls of his feet, hardly jostling Alison in the process, then started across the weed-filled yard toward her car.

"Tucker, for Pete's sake, this really is ridiculous." She paused. "But it is a rather gentlemanly thing to do," she added, giving him a sly glance.

"It is *not* a gentlemanly gesture, lady," he said firmly. "I don't want you poking holes in my lawn with those silly shoes of yours. Don't try to do some tricky number on me to convince me that I'm a gentleman who should have a gentleman's gentleman living under his roof, because it won't work. I live alone, I intend to continue living alone, and I won't be responsible for Mercer Martin or anyone else. Got that?"

Alison sighed. "Yes."

He set her on her feet next to her car. "Good. Remember it." He opened the car door. "Good-bye, Alison. I'll see you in a couple of days."

She looked up at him. "All right, Tucker," she said softly. "I'd . . . I'd appreciate it if you'd forget about those kisses we shared. I really don't know what came over me. It must have been the heat."

He grinned at her. "They were hot, all right, those kisses. No doubt about it."

Alison glared at him and slid into the driver's seat. Tucker closed the door, then stepped away and watched as she backed down the drive and the car disappeared from sight.

"No, beautiful Alison," he said quietly, "I can't—*won't*—be responsible for another person's life." He drew a deep, shuddering breath. "Not ever again."

Two

Late the next morning, Alison marched into her office and sank into the chair behind her desk with a sigh.

The senior Mr. Brinker, she thought, fuming, was a dud. She'd carefully explained Tucker Boone's demand that other arrangements had to be made for Mercer Martin, but Mr. Brinker had simply smiled that condescending smile of his and said he was sure Alison would bring the matter to a satisfactory conclusion for all concerned. What the heck did that mean? Besides the fact, of course, that Mr. Brinker had no intention of helping her find someplace else for Mercer to live. She was on her own, handling another ding-dong case for Brinker, Brinker, and Abbot.

"I can't stand it," Alison said to her pencil holder. "Fourteen months of these kinds of cases. *Fourteen months.* And what do I have? Custody battles over tulip bulbs and Tucker Boone."

Alison got to her feet and walked to the window to stare down at the bustling city below.

Tucker Boone. It was as though he'd climbed into the car with her and stuck like glue as she'd driven to her apartment. He'd been there through her entire evening, haunting her with the remembrances of his kisses, taunting her with his voice, his smile, his delicious body.

Alison moaned inwardly. She'd kissed a client. Unprofessional. Disgraceful. Incredible. Never in her life had she felt such instant, burning desire, such need and want. In Tucker's arms, she'd been aware of her own femininity, as though it were a newly discovered treasure to cherish. She was woman and Tucker was man. Together they were like nothing she'd ever known. Her body had hummed with sensuality while committing to memory every inch of Tucker Boone's body, which virtually shouted raw masculinity.

Tucker Boone, Alison's mind whispered. A lazy wanderer with no roots who made it clear that he lived for himself and wouldn't be responsible for anyone else—not even a quiet gentleman's gentleman—had kissed her senseless, then followed her right into her dreams for the entire night. If he knew how vivid those dreams had been, she wouldn't be able to face him again.

Why had Tucker had such an overwhelming effect on her? Alison asked herself. It was more than upsetting, it was a tad frightening. She didn't kiss her clients! And she certainly didn't keep company with lazy vagabonds who thought that total neglect of a home and property created "an earthy charm."

Well, whatever strange spell had fallen over her during the time spent with Tucker, she decided firmly, it was over. Done. Finished. From now on it was strictly business. She and Tucker would solve the problem concerning Mercer Martin, and that would be that. Case closed. She'd never see Tucker Boone again.

Never?

"Of course not," Alison said aloud. Tucker would pack up his hammock and move on to heaven only knew where. And she'd be in Houston at Brinker, Brinker, and Abbot, fighting custody battles over tulip bulbs.

How depressing.

"Hey, Alison," Nick said, coming into the office, "how did your meeting with Brinker go?"

She turned to face him. "It didn't. He just dumped Tucker Boone and Mercer Martin back into my lap, smiled that icky smile of his, and said he had all the faith in the world in me to straighten out the situation. I swear, Nick, if he would have patted me on the head, I would have screamed. Or maybe even punched him in the nose."

Nick chuckled. "Think positive. Being a junior partner of this prestigious firm will look very good on your résumé."

"Oh, really? Word is going to get out that I'm being given gofer cases. I'll be the laughingstock of the yuppie crowd, the standing joke in the after-hours bars where everyone goes. This outfit has got to give me some cases that mean something. I need a case that will allow me to show what I can do in a courtroom in front of a jury. It's been fourteen months, Nick. I'm entertaining serious thoughts of finding another position."

Nick leveled one hip onto the edge of Alison's desk. "No kidding? Well, it's up to you, but I think you're rushing it a bit. Whether you believe it or not, the experience you're getting here is very valuable. I know you don't like to hear this, Alison, but you've got to be patient. You're in such a hurry to conquer the world, and it isn't going to happen as fast as you'd like. Are your parents as impatient? Did you inherit this streak of full steam ahead, or learn it by watching them as you grew up?"

"No," she said, shaking her head. "I'm not like them at all. My mother is an artist, paints beautifully in oils. She gives her work away to people she likes. About ten years ago a gallery owner saw one of her pieces in a friend's home and approached my mother about the possibility of showing her work at his gallery. She said she wasn't interested in painting except for her own pleasure, and that she couldn't imagine her work hanging in a stranger's house. Lord, what a waste of talent. She could have been on her way to a brilliant career."

"To each his own," Nick said.

"I know, but . . . well, I'm very different from my parents, that's all. I love them, I truly do, and they love me, but we really don't understand each other. They feel I'm missing out on a great deal by not being married and having a child by now. We don't mean to pass judgment on each other's life-styles, but it's very difficult not to. We finally agreed it would be best to avoid the subject of career choices."

"What about your father?" Nick asked. "What does he do for a living?"

"He was a college professor."

"Was?"

"Was," she said, nodding. "Dr. Murdock was highly respected in the academic world, much published in the field of American history, and had tenure at Stanford."

"And?"

"He quit," Alison said, throwing up her hands. "I was eight years old at the time. My father had always wanted a large family, lots of children. For some unknown reason that the doctors could never figure out, there were no more babies after me. So my father walked away from Stanford and moved us here to Houston, where he'd been offered a job teaching second grade. Second grade! To be with the little ones, he always said. My mother thought it was the sweetest thing in the world. He's still there, teaching second grade. Such a waste of a wealth of knowledge about this country's history. I realize that elementary-school teachers are vitally important in the educational system, but my father is a near genius and has so much to offer on the college level."

"I see," Nick said thoughtfully. "You don't feel, I take it, that either of your parents lived up to their potential. But you intend to, and in record time—warp-factor ten."

Alison frowned. "You sound as though you don't approve."

"I didn't say that. I understand where you're coming from, but I do wonder if you aren't pushing yourself to make certain that you don't fall into the same pattern as your parents. How do you know, how can you be sure, what Alison Murdock really wants?"

"I know exactly what I want, Nick."

He slid off the desk and started across the room. "Do you?" he asked over his shoulder as he went through the doorway.

Alison stared after Nick, then wrapped her hands around her elbows in a protective gesture.

"Yes," she whispered, "I know. I'm going to be a fantastic trial attorney, one of the very best. I have the potential, and I intend to use it. Nothing is going to stop me." She paused. "Quit talking to yourself, Alison."

A shiver coursed through her, and Alison tightened her hold on her arms. The room suddenly seemed too quiet, too empty, as though daring her to use the solitude to look deep within herself. She felt disoriented, shaken, and terribly, terribly alone.

She was just tired. She hadn't slept well, thanks to Tucker Boone's uninvited presence in her dreams. Yes, she was tired—and frustrated—over the lack of challenging cases at Brinker, Brinker, and Abbot. And she was still off kilter because she'd kissed a client with the abandon of a wanton woman. She had to get herself back on course. With a decisive nod Alison crossed the room and sat down at her desk. She flipped open a file, then hesitated, her gaze drawn again to the empty doorway through which Nick had walked.

Nick didn't understand how she felt, she realized.

Nick Capoletti, like her parents, was content to be much less than he was capable of being. No one seemed to understand her need to achieve, to live up to her potential. A man like Tucker Boone— Alison blinked. "Go away, Tucker Boone," she said, flapping her hand in the air.

"Quit talking to yourself, Alison," Nick said, passing the doorway as he went down the hall.

"Oh, brother," Allison said, then buried her nose in the file.

Tucker slowly strolled toward the house from the barn, his hands shoved into the back pockets of his jeans. He'd ambled at his leisure across the entire fifteen acres of the property, seeing just what it was that he'd inherited from his often eccentric grandfather.

It was fine land, top-notch, Tucker mused. He'd seen healthy cattle and horses grazing on the neighboring mini-ranches, along with rich fields of alfalfa, grass, and hay. The house and barn were sound, well constructed, and needed only a few coats of paint to spruce them up. The corrals could be easily repaired. With a little money and a lot of labor, the entire place could become something a man would be proud to call his own.

Tucker stopped, squinting against the hot, glaring sun as he scanned the gently rolling hills of the land, then settling his gaze on the house.

A home, he thought. Not just a house but a home. Roots. A sense of permanence. He'd never wanted that before, had always been plagued by wanderlust, a need to move and keep going.

He'd taken after his parents in that respect, he knew, as they, too, had heeded the call of the wild when it whispered their names in a voice only they could hear. Their deaths during a mountain-climbing expedition years before had caused Tucker to seek out a dark, quiet place and cry tears of sadness. Yet he'd understood why they had been on that mountain, knew that its very existence had been the challenge they'd thrived on: the need to conquer the unknown. When his sorrow ebbed, he'd found solace in the knowledge that his parents had died as they had lived: taking on the next adventure. If only he could find that kind of inner peace about—

No, Tucker thought, shaking his head, he wasn't going to dwell on it now. He needed to focus on himself, determine why, after all these years, he was viewing this house and property he'd inherited from Jeremy Daniel Boone through eyes that saw it as a possible home, a place to settle down.

Over the past six months or so, he admitted, he'd sensed a change in himself, a nagging void that he'd ignored. It was as though he'd been searching for something just beyond his comprehension, a shadowy entity that refused to identify itself.

Tucker's eyes flickered over the land again. Was this what he'd been seeking? he wondered. Was he ready to come home? Even daring to consider the idea of staying in one spot for any length of time surprised him. He'd pictured himself living out his life on the move, never stopping anywhere for long. But he could no longer ignore the sense of emptiness within; he had to square off against it, find out what it was. Maybe his cagey grandfather had sensed in Tucker his need for roots.

"I don't know," Tucker said aloud. "Maybe. Maybe it *is* time."

He started walking toward the house again, deciding he'd had enough of the heat for now and envisioning a cold beer quenching his thirst. He'd make a list of things that needed tending to on the small ranch. Even if he discovered he was too restless to stay on, he had to spruce up the place before he could sell it. The house definitely needed painting. What it didn't need, for crying out loud, was a butler, a damn gentleman's gentleman. The pending arrival of Mercer Martin was as welcome as a toothache. Well, Alison would just have to deal with it.

He entered the kitchen, lifted a beer from the refrigerator, pulled the tab, and took a deep swallow. He leaned against the counter and rolled the can back and forth between the palms of his hands.

Alison.

A smile tugged at his lips. Alison Murdock was really something. Lord, she was beautiful, and those kisses they'd shared? More than once in the night he'd been awakened with a start, his heart thundering from the sensuous dream he'd been having about her. Desire had thrummed low, hot, and heavy in his body during the night and was starting to pull at him again right now at the mere vision in his mind of taking Alison into his arms. It had been a long time, if ever, since a woman had turned him inside out the way Alison had.

Alison.

Tucker sifted the sound of her name through his mind, liking it, deciding it was as pretty as the woman herself. She was a contradiction of sorts. One minute she was prim, proper, knocking herself out to appear professional. It was as though she had an image of what an attorney should be, and was attempting to cram herself into a mold that didn't quite fit her . . . as if she wanted to present an image of a person as stuffy, cool, and detached as old Brinker himself. But Alison didn't pull it off.

"Nope," he said, then drained the beer can.

He tossed the can into the sink, where it bounced once, then settled next to another. He wandered into the living room and stood statue-still, remembering Alison's laughter as it had resounded and echoed off the walls, filling the room to overflowing.

That was the real Alison, Tucker decided. And it had been the real Alison who had kissed him, allowed the passion within her to match his own. It had been Alison, the woman, not the would-be, hot-shot attorney, who had checked him out while he'd been pretending to be asleep in the hammock.

Tucker began to pull the sheets from the furniture, finding himself pleased with the style and quality of what he discovered. The house could be comfortable, attractive. A real home. For a family.

"Whoa," he said, then sprawled out on the sofa. A family? A wife, children? All looking to him for their welfare and happiness? No. No way. If he stayed on, he stayed alone. There'd be no wife, no kids, and there sure as hell wouldn't be a gentleman's gentleman who poured tea and made sandwiches with no crusts.

Tucker frowned. He was alone, he repeated in his mind, and he intended to remain so. But, well, he would admit he'd liked the way Alison had looked sitting in the living room. And he'd sure liked the sound of her laughter flitting through the air. And, oh, Lord, he could go for more of those kisses. Just kisses? Not a chance. He wanted to make love to Alison Murdock. His body tightened as the pictures accompanying his daydream became even more graphic, and he lunged to his feet.

"Dust this place, Boone," he said. "It's time to change the decor from earthy charm." He scooped up the pile of sheets on the floor. "And you get out of my head, Alison Murdock. You're driving me nuts."

Early the next morning Alison paced restlessly across her small living room, glancing often at her watch. She'd been up since dawn, due to the fact that she'd refused to spend another minute in that bed with Tucker Boone.

She was fuming. He had done it again—marched right smack-dab into her dreams, just as bold as you please. And any minute now he was going to show up in living, breathing Technicolor at her door. As if on cue, there was a knock at the door and Alison jumped. She took a steadying breath, smoothed the skirt of her yellow shirtwaist dress, and started across the room.

"If you don't act professional, Alison," she mumbled, "I'll strangle you."

She plastered a rather bored expression on her face and opened the door. And then she just stood there and stared at Tucker. She didn't speak, and wondered vaguely if she was still breathing.

Gorgeous Tucker Boone.

In dark slacks and a crisp white shirt open at the neck, his thick, sun-streaked hair neatly combed, his shoulders a mile wide, hips narrow, muscled thighs pressing against the material of his pants, his features ruggedly beautiful.

"Good morning, Alison," Tucker said quietly.

And he'd brought that sexy, rumbly voice with him, she thought wildly. He looked better than she remembered, even more virile and masculine than the Tucker who'd haunted her dreams.

"Alison?"

"What?" She blinked. "Oh! Come in, Tucker." She stepped back.

He entered and quickly crossed the room to put distance between them as she shut the door. He turned slowly to face her where she still stood by the door. Their eyes met. Neither spoke.

She looked like a spring flower in that dress, Tucker thought. She was a vision. He wanted to kiss her, hold her, feel her soft body pressed to his hard one. He wanted to taste her, inhale her aroma, evoke the passion within her to a raging fire directed at him. He wanted Alison Murdock like no woman he'd ever wanted before. All he had to do was cross that room, take her into his arms, and . . .

As though pulled by invisible strings, they started forward at the same moment. They met in the middle of the room, and Tucker gently framed Alison's face in his large hands.

"I'm going to kiss you," he said, his voice raspy.

"Yes," she whispered.

"I have to."

"Yes."

"Even though it's not a very good idea."

"Yes."

"You have a limited vocabulary."

"Yes."

"Dammit, Alison, what are you doing to me?"

"Waiting for you to kiss me, because if you don't, I'll dissolve, and I don't know what you're doing to me, either, but it's very scary, and I don't like it one little bit, and you're my client, and this is so-o-o unprofessional, but I—"

"Alison."

"Yes?"

"Shut up."

"Okay."

It was as though they'd waited an eternity for this kiss, had been anticipating it, savoring the thought of how it would be. Lips and tongues met urgently, hungrily, moving eagerly. A groan of pleasure rumbled up from Tucker's chest. A purr caught in Alison's throat.

He dropped his hands to her back to press her near as she lifted her arms to encircle his neck. It was better than the dreams of the night—it was real. It was taste and aromas and the feel of bodies nestled close; one ruggedly hard, one gently soft.

The kiss pushed reason and reality into oblivion and left only the ecstasy of what they were sharing. Passion soared. Want and need consumed them like a brushfire out of control.

Tucker lifted his lips only far enough to draw a

ragged breath. "I want you, Alison," he murmured, his voice gritty. "Lord, how I want to make love to you."

Of course he did, Alison thought dreamily—and she wanted him. She wanted to become one with him, not just at this moment but every day and every night, as time stretched into infinity. She wanted him now and for all her tomorrows.

"Let me love you, Alison," Tucker said. "Nothing matters except the way we feel right now. It was meant to be, this stolen time."

Stolen time? Alison's mind echoed. Stolen? That meant it wasn't really theirs, would have to be given back, wasn't something to keep. Tucker Boone, the vagabond, the wanderer, didn't believe in tomorrows. And her tomorrows were centered on her career, not on what might come to be between her and a special man. Oh, dear heaven, this was wrong. The wrong people, in the wrong place, wanting each other.

"No," she said, dropping her arms from his neck. She stepped back on trembling legs, forcing him to release her.

Tucker frowned. "Alison? What's the matter? We want each other. We're adults capable of making our own decisions. Why are you denying us when we both want this?"

"I don't have casual sex, Tucker," she said, hearing the shaky quality to her voice. "It has to be special, mean something, be important."

"Doesn't the fact that you've been on my mind since I met you mean something?" he said. "That's never happened to me before. It's as though you've been next to me every minute. I'd say that was very special." Lord, just listen to those words, he thought with disgust. He was pleading his case like a desperate kid. But, dammit, he meant what he said. Something different—and, yes, special—was happening between Alison and him. It wouldn't be casual sex, not by a long shot.

"I've thought about you, too, Tucker," she said, "but . . . No, this is wrong. I can't do this. No."

"Why not?"

"Because *we're* wrong, don't you see? This isn't the time in our lives for this. We're operating on different planes, walking different roads."

He ran his hand over the back of his neck. "That sounds like a poem or something. I don't understand what you're trying to say."

Alison pressed her hands to her flushed cheeks for a moment, then grasped her elbows in a tight hold. "Tucker, you told me that you move around a lot, that you're a wanderer and you exist alone to the point that you don't even have room in your life for a gentleman's gentleman."

"Well, yes, but I've been thinking that maybe it's time that I—"

"And I," Alison rushed on, interrupting him, "am concentrating totally on my career. I don't know why you've had such a startling effect on me, but I plan to ignore it from now on. I simply don't have time for this, for us."

Tucker narrowed his eyes. "I don't like the way that sounds. This isn't a schedule for a football game. Dammit, Alison, something is happening between us!"

"Well, it's just going to have to stop happening," she said, planting her hands on her hips. "You're going to pack up your hammock and shuffle off to Buffalo, and my future is centered on becoming the best attorney I can possibly be. The fact that I can't stop thinking about you, and when you kiss me I want . . . well, it isn't going to be allowed to matter."

"I see," he said slowly. "Your career is the most important thing in your life."

"Yes."

He nodded. "So, even if there's something unique, rare, and very special happening between us, you'll just push it aside and continue on the road to your goal."

"Well, you're making it sound a tad cold and unfeeling, but, yes, that's how it is. That's how it has to be."

Tucker crossed his arms over his chest. "Well, I guess you spelled that out loud and clear. Ready to go to the airport?"

"What? Oh, yes, of course. Tucker, I'm sorry if I led you to believe that I was prepared to go further than just kissing you. I'm still in shock that I kissed you at all. I don't seem to behave true to form around you, but it won't happen again. We understand each other now."

"Yep," he said, rocking back on the balls of his feet. "We certainly do."

"You're not angry, are you?"

"Me? Do I look mad, darlin'?"

Alison squinted up at him. "I don't know. I can't read your expression at all. It's just sort of . . . blank."

"Don't worry about a thing," he said pleasantly.

"Let's get going. The traffic is really heavy this morning."

"I'll get my purse." She eyed him warily for another long moment, then started toward the bedroom.

Angry? Tucker asked himself. He'd gladly wring her beautiful neck! She was dusting him off, dismissing whatever it was that had sprung up between them, just the way she might flick away a pesty fly. She didn't have *time* for this, for him? Well, they'd see about that. He'd never been so insulted in his life. And never in his life had he wanted a woman with such aching need as he did Alison Murdock. None of this was going to be allowed to matter? Ha! *He* wanted to know exactly what it all meant, and he intended to find out. *He* controlled his life, not some whisper of a woman who could be blown over by a strong wind. Alison Murdock was dealing with Tucker Boone, by damn.

"All set," Alison said, coming out of the bedroom. "Are you ready?"

"Oh, yes, darlin', I'm ready," Tucker said, nodding.

Why did she get the feeling that she was missing something? Alison wondered as they left the apartment. A message, an underlying . . . something that she couldn't quite put her finger on. No, she was just imagining it. Tucker had listened to what she'd said and had understood. No problem.

There would be, she knew, no more of those mind-boggling kisses. None. He'd calmly accepted her ending their physical involvement. Calmly accepted it, yes. She frowned. Not the most flattering reaction in the world. The man could have argued his case a bit more. Oh, for Pete's sake, she was being ridiculous.

Everything was now as it should be, had to be—she realized that. What she couldn't figure out was why she felt as though she were a breath away from bursting into tears.

The car that Tucker had rented was a bright red sedan with a white interior. He tuned the radio to a country-western station, set the volume on high, and tapped his fingers on the steering wheel to the rhythm of the music as he weaved expertly through the surging traffic.

"Tucker," Alison finally said as they approached the airport. "Tucker!"

"Huh?" he said, snapping his head around to look at her.

"Watch the road."

"What?"

Alison reached over and turned off the radio as Tucker redirected his attention to the traffic.

"Hey," he said, "that was a great song."

"A loud song. I wanted to ask you when I should tell Mercer what the situation is. Should I do it right away, or let him relax a bit? Or tell him after we get back to the house? What do you think?"

"What did Brinker have to say about all of this?"

"He expressed his confidence in my ability to handle it."

"So he isn't looking around for a place for Mercer to go?"

"No, it's up to me."

"That's interesting. Look, let's play it by ear. Don't say anything to Mercer until I give you the word. The old guy has had a long flight, plus he may be grieving for my grandfather. They were together a long time. We'll see what kind of shape he's in."

"That's very thoughtful of you, Tucker," Alison said, smiling.

"I'm a very thoughtful person, ma'am."

"But you're not a gentleman," Alison said, still smiling.

Tucker hooted. "Nope, not me."

"All right, Mr. Thoughtful, I won't say anything to Mercer until you and I hold a secret conference."

"Check," Tucker said. He was buying himself some time, he mused. He needed time to sort through the jumble in his mind. He had to find out if he wanted to settle down in one place after all these years. He had to find out just what it was that was happening between Alison and him. He had to find out what it might mean to him, a man who wanted no part of being responsible for another person.

If Alison whisked Mercer off to someplace else right away, it would be difficult for Tucker to see her. This had to be handled with finesse, expertise, until he got the answers to his questions. At least old Brinker wouldn't be sticking his nose in.

The computer screens on the wall in the airport indicated that Mercer's flight was on time. Alison hurried to keep up with Tucker's long-legged stride as they headed for the assigned gate.

Tucker was parting the crowd like the Red Sea, she thought. People just automatically got out of his way. The women were certainly doing their share of double takes as Tucker moved by them. But who could blame them? He was incredibly good-looking, and built like a dream. He'd appeal to the high-society gals, who would adore the chance to smooth Tucker's rough edges. He'd appeal to those in faded jeans and shirts, seeing Tucker as one of their own. He would, in fact, appeal to any female who didn't have one foot in the grave.

"This is it," Tucker said, glancing up at a large sign. "The passengers are coming through that door over there."

"It just occurred to me that I have no idea what to say to a gentleman's gentleman."

Tucker shrugged. "Beats me. I heard him say 'More tea?' a couple of times, but that's about it."

"Will you recognize him?"

"Believe me, you can't miss him. He's . . . hey, there he is. Now, I ask you, is that authentic or what? Dark suit with vest, a bowler hat . . . even a walking stick. Across the way there, darlin', you see a gentleman's gentleman, a butler in his purest form."

"Oh, Tucker, he's wonderful, absolutely adorable," Alison said, her eyes sparkling. "He looks like Abraham Lincoln."

Tucker chuckled, then raised a hand to catch Mercer's attention. The tall, thin man made his way toward them, no readable expression on his face when he stopped in front of them.

"Well, Mercer," Tucker said, "welcome to America. This is Alison Murdock."

"Mum," Mercer said, inclining his head slightly toward Alison.

"Hello," she said, smiling. "I hope you'll like it here."

"Thank you, mum," Mercer said.

"Well . . . um . . . Mercer," Tucker said, "why don't we get your luggage and split?"

"Split, sir?" Mercer said.

"Leave. Go," Tucker said.

"Oh, of course, Master Boone. Very good, sir."

"Right," Tucker said, sliding a quick look at Alison. She smiled at him. "Come on."

Mercer didn't move.

"Mercer?" Tucker said.

"I'm waiting for the madam to precede me, sir. She really should . . . split before I do."

"Thank you, Mercer," Alison said, slipping her arm around Tucker's. "You're most kind."

The trio started off, with Mercer bringing up the rear.

"I'm not going to survive this," Tucker said under his breath. "I can feel myself aging already."

Alison laughed in delight.

Three

Tucker didn't turn the radio on in the car. There was no sparkling conversation, and the trip from the airport to the ranch was made in total silence.

Mercer sat ramrod-stiff in the backseat, his bowler hat resting on his knees. He still had no readable expression on his face. Alison glanced often at him, but he gave no clue as to what reaction he was having to the new things he was seeing.

He was in his middle fifties, Alison knew from the information she'd been given, but he had one of those ageless faces. His dark hair was generously sprinkled with gray, but that was the only clue to his years.

He was so . . . stoic, she mused. So controlled. What would it take to make Mercer Martin smile? But he was probably exhausted from his long trip, and perhaps still mourning the death of his longtime friend and employer, Jeremy Daniel Boone. Poor Mercer. How difficult it must be to be uprooted and find himself in a strange country at his age. Oh, heavens, how was she going to tell him that he was not going to be staying on with Tucker?

"Home," Tucker said, turning into the driveway and bringing Alison from her troubled thoughts. "Don't judge it as it looks now, Mercer. The place needs a bit of sprucing up."

A *lot* of sprucing up, Alison thought, getting out of the car. She was surprised that Mr. Earthy Charm Boone recognized that fact.

"Let's go inside," Tucker said. "I'll get your luggage later, Mercer."

"Oh, no, Master Boone," Mercer said, "I'll see to my cases." He got out of the car and went to stand by the trunk.

"Right," Tucker muttered, getting out of the car.

"We'll all help with the luggage," Alison said brightly. "Then we can have a cool drink. You must be very warm in that suit, Mercer. You can change into something more casual."

"Casual, madam?" he asked.

"Well, sure. You know, take off your jacket, vest, tie, put on a short-sleeved shirt and . . ." She paused. "No, huh?"

"This is my usual attire, mum," he said. "It wouldn't be proper for me to wear anything else."

"Oh, I see," Alison said.

"Could we go inside?" Tucker asked gruffly. "It's getting hot as hell out here." He opened the trunk, lifted out two large suitcases, and started toward the house. "I fixed the front steps," he called over his shoulder. "Just tromp through the weeds and let's get out of this heat."

Mercer took two more suitcases, and Alison was left to close the trunk and bring up the rear. She sighed. This wasn't going very well, she thought. Mercer was as stiff as a board, Tucker was getting crabby, and she felt like Little Mary Sunshine, flitting around trying to ease the building tension.

In the living room, Alison smiled in delight when she saw the sparkling clean room and the absence of the sheets covering the furniture.

"Oh, my, doesn't everything look nice?" she said. "You've certainly worked hard, Tucker."

"Mmm," he said, scowling. "Come on, Mercer. I'll show you to your room."

"Very good, sir."

As Tucker and Mercer disappeared down the hall, Alison sank onto the sofa. She was getting a headache, she realized, gently massaging her temples. She'd *earned* the right to have a headache.

Tucker came striding back into the room and headed for the kitchen. "Want a beer, Alison?" he said as he passed her.

"No thank you." She got to her feet and hurried after him. "Do you have any more lemonade?"

In the kitchen, Tucker yanked a beer can and the pitcher of lemonade out of the refrigerator. He reached for ice cubes and thunked several into a glass with more force than was necessary.

"I'll pour it," Alison said quickly. "Where's Mercer?"

Tucker pulled the tab on the beer can and took several swallows. "Unpacking. Didn't I tell you that he was odd? He reminds me of an undertaker in an old movie."

"Tucker, keep your voice down. Mercer is tired from his long trip. Besides, you have to realize that this is a major change for someone his age—for anyone, really. He'll loosen up once he's settled in and gets used to things." She paused and frowned. "Won't he?"

"No. I saw him at my grandfather's, remember? He's always like this."

"Doesn't he ever smile?"

"I don't think a gentleman's gentleman is allowed to smile. It's taught to them in basic training, or whatever. Alison, this is Texas—laid-back, easygoin' Texas. Nobody is going to want an undertaker skulking around in the shadows."

Alison laughed. "He's not *that* bad."

"Yes he is." Tucker drained the can and tossed it into the sink.

"Well, we'll simply have to retrain him, that's all. He agreed to come here. I'm sure he'll be receptive to change, to learning how to adapt to his new environment. We'll help him. Yes, that's exactly what we'll do."

We, Tucker thought. She kept saying *we*. "That sounds like it has possibilities," he said slowly.

"Sure. Of course, you'd have to stay here a while until we accomplished our goal, prepared Mercer to go live with someone else."

"I . . . um . . . I could hang around for a while," he said, looking directly into her eyes.

"Yes," she said softly. She blinked and cleared her

throat as a curl of heat fluttered low in her body. "Tucker, just what is it that you do when you go off to do whatever it is that you do? Did that make sense? What I mean is, just what do you do?"

He shrugged. "Check up on things."

She leaned slightly toward him. "Things?"

"Yeah, things. Stuff that I own. I hang around, work with my crews, go over records with my top men, make sure everything is under control, then move on to the next . . . thing."

"Like what?"

"I've got a couple of gold mines in South America, some offshore oil wells here and there, part ownership in a Las Vegas casino, plus a few other odds and ends."

Alison's eyes widened. "You're kidding."

"Nope. I inherited the gold mines when my parents died. The rest I've put together on my own. Now I've got this place. I'm the last of the Boones, the only one left."

"I had no idea that you owned—I mean, I thought you were a . . . a . . ."

"A bum?" He chuckled. "A hobo who just wandered around the world?"

"Not quite that bad, but sort of. It sounds to me, Tucker Boone," she said, planting her hands on her hips, "that you're every bit as eligible to have a gentleman's gentleman as your grandfather was."

"The difference is," he said, raising his hands, "I don't want one."

"Right. You live alone and want to remain alone."

"True." He nodded. "But," he added quickly, "I

think that out of respect for Jeremy Daniel Boone we owe it to Mercer to get him ready to fit into a high-society Houston household. I agree to your plan, Alison. We'll whip old Mercer into shape together, you and me."

Together, Alison thought. What a lovely, warm sound that word suddenly had. Alison and Tucker, together. Oh, heavens, she was being so foolish, should be putting as much distance as possible between herself and Tucker instead of glowing in anticipation of their joint project of Mercer.

No, now, wait a minute, she told herself, she could handle this. She was a mature adult and knew that it was a temporary arrangement, that Tucker eventually would leave. She wouldn't be hurt, because she had all the facts. And it wasn't pulling her from the road leading to her career goals because Tucker was her client, and Mercer part of an assigned case. Fine. Everything was under control.

"Alison? Are you in there?" Tucker asked.

"What? Oh, yes, I was just thinking. This is going to work splendidly, Tucker."

"Good. I'm going to fix the place up, you know. Create the proper atmosphere so that Mercer will feel more at ease and get used to an American home. That will help him when he goes to work for someone else."

"Excellent," Alison said, smiling. In the next instant she frowned. "Are we going to say anything to Mercer yet about this being a temporary arrangement?"

"No," Tucker said quickly. "No, I've decided he's had enough upheaval in his life for now. He lived in that drafty castle with my grandfather for thirty years. Mercer needs a chance to relax and adjust before we spring anything else on him."

"You're really very thoughtful, Tucker."

He grinned at her. "Just don't get carried away and accuse me of being a gentleman."

"Heaven forbid," Alison said in mock horror. "I wouldn't dream of it."

Tucker chuckled. "I should hope not."

"Tucker, is your phone fixed yet?"

"Yeah."

"Good. I need to call Nick."

Tucker stiffened. "Nick? Who's Nick?"

Alison moved around him and went to the telephone on the kitchen wall. Tucker was right behind her.

"Who's Nick?" he repeated.

Alison lifted the receiver and began to dial. "The paralegal assigned to me. He's my right hand, my secretary, researcher, all that stuff."

"You have a male secretary?"

"Not exactly. Well, yes, I guess so. Nick is a paralegal. He does a little bit of everything."

"How old is this joker?" Tucker asked, scowling at the back of her head.

"Thirty. Hello? Trudy? This is Alison. May I speak with Nick, please? Thank you."

"Thirty?" Tucker repeated. "You have a thirty-year-old male— Is he married?"

"No. Nick? . . . Alison. Anything I should know? . . . Yes. . . . Really? That's wonderful. . . . Oh? What time? . . . All right, I'll be there. Thank you, Mr. Capoletti. 'Bye." She replaced the receiver.

"Capoletti?" Tucker roared.

Alison jumped in surprise, then turned to face him, nearly bumping into his chest.

"The guy is a hot-blooded Italian?"

"Tucker, what is your problem?" Alison asked, frowning up at him.

"Nothing," Tucker said, running his hand over the back of his neck. "It just sounds weird, that's all, your having a man working for you. A thirty-year-old Italian man."

"Paralegals are very common in large law firms. They come in all ages, shapes, and sizes."

"What kind of shape is Capoletti in?" Tucker asked, still scowling.

Alison laughed. "He's a heartbreaker. If it weren't for his photographic memory, I doubt that he could keep track of all of his women."

Tucker clenched his jaw so tightly that his teeth ached.

"Where's my lemonade? I poured it but never drank it." She glanced around, then walked over to the counter. "Nick had great news for me. The custody case over the tulip bulbs was dropped. The couple has reconciled and are planning a cruise as a second honeymoon."

"That's nice," Tucker said absently. Dammit, what was wrong with him? He could feel a knot of fury as big as a bowling ball in his gut. If he didn't know better, he'd think that the existence of Nick Capoletti in Alison's life had caused him to register a flash of jealousy. No way. Tucker Boone jealous? Never happened. Women had tried to make him jealous in the past, but he'd waved it off and gone on to greener pastures. No, he wasn't jealous of Capoletti.

"Okay?" Alison was saying.

"What?" Tucker said, snapping his head around to look at her.

"I have a staff meeting at three. I'll need you to drive me into town in time for me to get my car and be at the office by then."

"Yeah, sure."

"Thank you. Tucker, do you think you should go check on Mercer? Maybe he doesn't know what you want him to do after he unpacks. He could be sitting in his room, not certain if he should come out."

"Oh, I didn't think of that." He paused. "What do I want him to do?"

"Well, it's nearly lunchtime, but Mercer has to be exhausted. Instead of having him prepare lunch, why don't you tell him that his duties won't start until tomorrow?"

"Good idea. That will postpone the sandwiches with no crusts for another day." Tucker strode from the room.

Alison laughed softly, then carried her glass of lemonade into the living room. She wandered around, looking at the plush, expensive furniture.

It really was a magnificent room, she mused. The entire house would be fantastic when it was fixed up. There was a warmth to the place, a sense of welcome. She'd decorated her tiny apartment in mint green and pale yellow, thinking it would appear cooler in the Houston summer weather. This room was done in dark wood and rich, vibrant colors; earth tones with splashes of bright accent colors in throw pillows and wall hangings. It should feel oppressive because of the heat, but it didn't. It was homey. She liked it here, in Tucker's house.

Temporary house, temporary home, she added quickly. She mustn't forget that. All of this, everything, was just temporary.

"Okay," Tucker said, coming back into the room. "You were right. Mercer was waiting to find out what I wanted him to do next. He was sitting in the rocker in his room, trying not to fall asleep."

"Oh, that poor man," Alison said. "Think how strange this all must seem to him, Tucker. He must feel so lost."

Tucker frowned and nodded. "Well, he's going to get some sleep now. I told him there was nothing for him to do today because you and I were going into town for lunch, and I wouldn't be back until late."

"You won't? Be back until late?" Alison said. Why? Did he have a date? Had there been time for Tucker to meet someone in Houston? Who was she kidding? Whenever Tucker walked, breathed, moved across a room, women paid attention, sent out signals that said, "Yoo-hoo, gorgeous man, I'm available." Oh, darn, her stomach hurt at the very thought of Tucker being with another woman.

"I have a lot to take care of," Tucker said. "I plan to do some of the work around this place myself, but some I'll hire others to do. I have supplies to buy, arrangements to make for crews."

Alison smiled. "That's nice. Yes, I guess you will be late getting back, won't you? Perfect. Mercer can have a good rest without feeling he should have been doing something that a gentleman's gentleman does for his gentleman. Not that you're a gentleman, of course. I certainly wouldn't imply such a thing. Goodness, no, I—"

"Alison," Tucker interrupted, raising an eyebrow, "why are you babbling?"

Her eyes widened. "Babbling? Me? Don't be absurd. An attorney never babbles. We're articulate, choose all our words very carefully, make every sentence count."

He chuckled. "Is that a fact?"

She sniffed indignantly. "It certainly is." She'd been babbling, she knew it, felt like an idiot, but had no intention of admitting it. "Are you really planning on taking me out to lunch?"

"Sure, darlin'. We'll go to a nice restaurant that's air-conditioned."

"We can discuss our strategy for turning Mercer into a Texas gentleman's gentleman."

"No, not today," Tucker said, shaking his head. "Mercer stays on hold until tomorrow. Let's go. I'm hungry, now that I really think about it."

"Yes, me too," Alison said, smiling. Her stomach, she realized, no longer hurt, not one bit.

The restaurant that Tucker chose was cool and inviting, with a sparkling, splashing fountain in the middle of the large room and a multitude of hanging plants. Alison ordered a chef's salad, and Tucker decided on a steak sandwich with a double order of cottage fries. Their lunches were placed quickly in front of them, and they ate in silence for several minutes.

"Tucker," Alison said finally, "may I ask you something? It's really none of my business, so don't feel you have to answer."

"Fair enough. What's the question?"

Alison chased an elusive cherry tomato across her salad, then gave up the attempt to spear it with her fork. She looked at Tucker.

"Well, you said that you were the last of the Boones. Some men would want to see to it that the name was carried on. Yet you're adamant about wishing to remain alone, not responsible for anyone but yourself. I just wondered why you felt so strongly about the subject."

Tucker leaned back in his chair and stared out the window. Seconds ticked by. Alison watched him intently, seeing the muscle ticking in his jaw.

"You're right," he said, not looking at her, "it's none of your business."

Now her heart hurt, Alison thought. Tucker's voice was so cold, flat, and angry. She knew it was none of her business, but having him tell her in that voice, without even looking at her, really did make her heart hurt.

"I'm sorry," she said softly. "I didn't mean to pry." She busied herself chasing the cherry tomato with her fork again, but it rolled away like a soccer ball.

Tucker slowly turned his head to look at her. "Hey, I'm the one who's sorry," he said quietly. "I didn't mean to jump down your throat. I just . . . don't want to talk about it, okay?"

She met his gaze and managed a small smile. "Of

course. I won't mention it again." She paused. "So! What color are you going to paint the outside of the house?"

"Alison, why is your career the only thing you're willing to focus on in your life?"

She blinked. "Where did that question come from?"

"Under the heading of, 'none of my business,' like your question about me. You don't have to answer."

"I only hate to answer because I come across as standing in judgment of my parents and anyone else who doesn't live up to his or her potential. I'm not passing judgment, I just know what *I* need to do. I want to be the best trial attorney that I'm capable of being."

"Your parents don't respect that?"

She sighed. "Not exactly. They think I should settle for less career-wise and have a family. Both of them had incredible career possibilities and chose to pull back, not reach their potential. They don't understand me. I love them, they love me, but on the issue of ambition we're poles apart. We simply don't discuss it anymore. It's better that way."

"I see. Your parents have a philosophy of slowing down, taking time to smell the flowers, that sort of thing."

She leaned toward him. "They have gifts they're not using, Tucker. Nick is another one like that. He's so brilliant, could be an outstanding attorney, but he's content to be a paralegal. It's a waste, all of it."

"Are they happy? Your parents? This Capoletti guy?"

"Well, yes, they seem to be."

"Doesn't that count for something?"

"Of course it does. But for me to be happy I have to do things my way."

"And no one seems to understand your desire to be all that you can be."

"Yes, that's about how it stacks up. So, go ahead, express your opinion. Tell me how I have tunnel vision about my career, how I'm missing out on a lot of living by concentrating on my goals. Lay it all on me, Tucker. Heaven knows everyone else has. Nick says I have no patience, that I'm in too big of a rush to accomplish what I want. Well? Don't you want to add your two cents' worth?"

Tucker squinted at the ceiling for a long moment before looking at her again. "What I think . . ." he began.

"Here it comes," Alison muttered.

". . . is that I should take bets on whether or not you're ever going to catch that tomato you're doing battle with there."

"What?"

"Forget it. You've got lousy wrist action. There's an art to spearing cherry tomatoes, darlin'. You need practice. In the meantime"—he reached across the table, plucked the tomato from the salad, and held it close to her lips as he leaned toward her—"open up."

Alison was so stunned by Tucker suddenly changing the direction of the conversation that she opened her mouth like a baby bird. He popped the tomato in, then slid his callused thumb slowly, sensuously, along her lower lip.

"Enjoy . . . your tomato," he said, his voice low and rumbly.

Alison assumed that she'd chewed and swallowed the sweet little tomato because it was no longer in her mouth. She was gazing into the depths of Tucker's blue eyes as he continued to lean toward her, and the room and noise surrounding them seemed to fade into a hazy mist.

Tucker shifted his gaze to her lips, then back to her eyes. She felt as though he'd actually kissed her, as though she could feel and taste his lips on hers.

"Oh, Tucker," she said, hardly more than a whisper.

With every ounce of willpower he could muster, Tucker slowly moved back. He wanted to slip his hand to the nape of Alison's neck and pull her close, kiss her slightly parted lips, meet her tongue, savor her taste. The blood pounded low in his body, his arousal heavy, heated, aching with the want of her.

Lord above, he thought incredulously, in the middle of a restaurant? This woman was a witch! No, this woman was Alison, and he might as well face it; his life was undergoing a major change. And like everything else he'd run up against in his travels that was new and different, he intended to meet this head-on.

The spell that Alison Murdock was casting over him was, admittedly, scaring the shorts off of him, but he'd stand his ground, see what it all meant, then deal with the facts as they became clear to him. And if she didn't quit looking at him like that, he was going to crawl across that table and haul her into his arms.

He cleared his throat roughly. "Alison—" He stopped when he realized he'd used up the entire supply of air in his lungs.

"Yes, Tucker?" she said, a dreamy quality to her voice.

"Eat your lettuce," he said gruffly, then shifted his attention to his plate.

Alison looked at her salad as though she'd never seen it before in her life. What had happened? she asked herself frantically. It was like being transported up and away to a lovely place that had contained only the two of them. She hadn't wanted to return from that place, had wanted only Tucker, all of him, had wanted to make love with this man, focus only on him and what they would share.

This was so frightening, she thought. She couldn't see the clearly defined road to her goals from that place and hadn't cared. The very essence of who she was had been centered on Tucker.

If she lost her footing on her road, she knew, she'd never find it again. She couldn't, wouldn't, allow that to happen. Nothing and no one would stop her from reaching her goals. No one, not even the magnificent Tucker Boone.

"Alison, don't," Tucker said quietly.

She lifted her head to look at him questioningly. "Pardon me?"

"Don't look so frightened, like a timid rabbit about to bolt. I'm not going to hurt you."

"You don't understand," she said, her voice shaky.

He trapped her hand with his on top of the table. "Don't lump me into that group of people you're so positive don't understand you. I heard what you said; I listened carefully. I know your career is important to you, and there's nothing wrong with that. But it doesn't mean there isn't room in your life for me, for us, time to discover what this is between us. We owe it to ourselves to find out what this is."

"No," she said, shaking her head and pulling her hand free. "I don't want to know. I can't let it matter. I'm giving myself some stolen time with you while we help Mercer, and maybe even doing that is wrong. I don't know. I do know it's temporary."

"While we help Mercer . . ." he repeated, narrowing his eyes.

Alison fiddled with her napkin, no longer able to look directly at him. "Yes," she murmured.

"I see."

She folded the napkin into a fan. "You'll be leaving after Mercer is settled in with someone else, anyway, so . . ." She shrugged.

"What if I stayed?" he asked, his voice low.

She snapped her head up to look at him. "You wouldn't do that. You travel, go from place to place to check on your oil wells, and gold mines, and whatever else you own. Why would you stay on here?"

"Maybe, just maybe, you understand, it's time I settled down."

Alison smacked the table with her hand. "Don't you dare!" She plunked her elbow down on the table and rested her forehead in her hand. "Oh, ignore me, I'm falling apart."

Tucker chuckled. Alison lifted her head and glared at him.

"Whoa, now," he said, raising one hand. "Don't

get in a snit. This is very simple, really." Ha! It was the most confusing, complicated situation he'd ever been in. "It's clear as a bell." Lord, what a bunch of bull.

"It is?" She paused. "It certainly is not."

"Sure, it is, darlin'." He folded his arms loosely over his chest and smiled at her. "We're attracted to each other." No joke. "But because of your career plans, you're only in this for the short haul. Temporarily—to quote you, Counselor. Whatever this is between us will end when Mercer has been transformed from an English undertaker into a Texas butler. Correct?"

"Well . . . yes," Alison said, frowning slightly.

"Check. That is *your* half of the conditions heretofore set forth regarding our relationship. That's legal jargon, darlin'. You ought to be able to grab that easy enough. Now then, we come to *my* half of the partnership, per se."

"Tucker, would you knock off the legalese and just make your point?"

"Okay. Listen up. You can't call all of the shots here, Alison, because I'm involved in this too. You're putting the time limit on us, so I'm laying down the conditions of how we'll operate during that time." Go for it, Boone. "If I want to kiss you, I'll kiss you. If I want to hold you in my arms"—he leaned toward her—"I'll hold you close, nestled to me, my hands moving here, there, and everywhere."

"Oh, good Lord," Alison whispered.

He was dying just talking about it. "That's how it will be. Fair is fair—we each have a voice in this. I'll accept your terms if you'll accept mine. I realize those kisses won't matter a whole helluva lot to you because your goals, the road to your career, is the most important thing in your life. Fine. See? Clear as a bell. Do we have a deal?"

"I'm not sure that—"

Tucker grabbed her hand and shook it. "Deal. Hey, it's getting late. We'd better get a move on." He signaled to the waitress. "I'm going to paint the barn red, like a barn should be. The house? What do you think of tan with dark brown trim? Of course, the corrals need fixing, and those I'll do white . . . ."

Tucker's words became nothing more than a buzz, like a swarm of bees, as Alison attempted to sift through the jumble in her mind.

Deal? her mind echoed. She hadn't agreed to what Tucker had said, had she? They'd see each other only for as long as it took to shape up Mercer Martin, and during that time Tucker could kiss the living daylights out of her? She'd agreed to that? No, she hadn't. Had she?

The next thing that Alison was totally aware of was being shoveled into Tucker's car. He turned the radio up full blast on the country-western station and drove to her apartment building.

"I'll just drop you off here," he said. "I've got a lot to do, you know." He brushed his lips over hers. " 'Bye. Talk to you later."

"Oh, yes, fine," she said, then got out of the car and closed the door.

Tucker drove away quickly, glancing once in the rearview mirror to see Alison still standing on the sidewalk. He took a deep breath, let it out slowly, then wiped a line of sweat off his brow with his thumb.

That had been tense, he thought, touch and go, but he'd pulled it off. Alison looked like she was in a fog. But he'd gotten the time he'd needed to find his answers, and Alison couldn't keep him at arm's length. Because, oh, yes, he intended to kiss her, and hold her, and he'd just see if none of it mattered to her.

But, damn, he thought suddenly, what if it didn't matter to her and he found out that Alison was a very important part of his life?

"Easy, Boone," he said. "This calls for steady nerves and a brilliant brain. So far you're doing fine."

Tucker began to hum along with a tune, tapping his fingers on the steering wheel as he drove.

Alison still had not moved minutes after Tucker had driven away.

"This isn't a bus stop, dear," an elderly woman said. "It's down closer to the corner. Are you lost?"

"What?" Alison said. "Lost? Oh, no, I'm just a tad confused."

"Can I help you in some way?"

"You're very kind, but no, you can't help me. I have a sneaky suspicion that I'm a hopeless case. 'Bye." She hurried toward her car.

"Poor little thing," the woman said. "She's nuttier than a fruitcake."

As Alison drove to the office she decided she wasn't in such bad shape, after all. Tucker had agreed to the temporary status of their relationship, and she was to enjoy his delicious kisses in the interim. Her future was still secure, as her road was once again very clearly defined. Mercer would be helped in the process, and a good time would be had by all. There really was nothing to be frightened of, because a deal was a deal, and she and Tucker had even shaken hands on it like true-blue Texans. Yes, now that she was able to sort it all through, she could see that everything was fine, under control.

With a decisive nod Alison tuned the radio to a country-western station and began to hum along with the tune.

It never occurred to her that she really didn't care for country-western music.

Four

Alison watched as the other members of the law firm of Brinker, Brinker, and Abbot filed out of the room. She snapped her briefcase closed and got to her feet. The senior Mr. Brinker had sat at the head of the gleaming mahogany table during the staff meeting and was now gathering his notes.

"Mr. Brinker," Alison said, "may I have a word with you, please?" She picked up her briefcase and walked to the end of the long table.

"Certainly, Alison," Mr. Brinker said. "Please sit down."

She sat in the chair nearest him. "Sir, I wanted to speak to you regarding the cases being assigned to me."

"You're doing very well, Alison. I'm most pleased with your progress since you've been with us. Your clients have had very flattering things to say about you."

"Thank you, sir, but my point is that I feel I'm ready for more challenging work."

"You have a very important case right now, my dear, in the carrying out of Jeremy Daniel Boone's addendum to his will. Jeremy Boone was a longtime client of this firm, as well as my friend, and I personally want to know that his final wishes were met. From what you explained during the staff meeting, you're facing a tremendous challenge in preparing Mercer Martin to be ready to fit into Houston society in a home other than Tucker Boone's. Yes, indeed, a tremendous challenge. You've cleared up your other pending cases and can now concentrate on seeing Jeremy Daniel Boone's final wishes through to their proper end. It was because of your report here today that I didn't assign you any new cases. Your energies can be centered on the subject at hand."

"Mr. Brinker, I'm capable of much more than helping Tucker Boone with Mercer Martin. I fully expected to be given another case today, and I do feel very strongly that I'm ready for something more substantive. Jeff Baker has been here a shorter time than I have, and he was given a trial case, defending a man on assualt-and-battery charges. That's the third trial case Jeff has had. I've had none."

"Jeff Baker has a natural flair for the courtroom, Alison. He was meant to be a trial lawyer. He has a spellbinding effect on a jury. Every attorney must find his place, what it is that he's most proficient at. Your detail work is excellent, and you do extremely well in closed cases in judges' chambers."

Alison stiffened. "What are you saying, Mr. Brinker?"

He smiled at her. "That you're excellent on a one-to-one basis. Excellent. I'm sure Mercer Martin will respond wholeheartedly to your assistance. As for a jury"—he frowned and shook his head—"well, not everyone is meant to be a trial lawyer. You don't, shall we say, command the authority needed for that area of the law. That is the beauty of our profession, Alison. There is a place for everyone and his own expertise."

"But my dream is to become a trial lawyer, Mr. Brinker," Alison said, feeling the color drain from her face. "I have the potential to be one of the finest trial—"

"No, my dear," Mr. Brinker said, interrupting gently, "you don't. When I take on a new, young lawyer fresh from school as I did you, Jeff, and a multitude before you over the years, I study their records very carefully. I take great pride in bringing along the ones just starting out. I have a reputation for knowing and sensing the real potential of my fledglings. You are sensitive and caring. Alison, you don't have the dynamic personality needed to take charge of an entire courtroom arena."

"That's not true," Alison said, her voice trembling. "That's my goal, where my road is leading. I'm going to be a trial lawyer."

"No, Alison," he said quietly, "you're not. You have much to offer this firm and the citizens of Houston, but not as a trial lawyer. You're an asset to us, and I hope you'll be with us for many years. But you must devote yourself to where your talents lie. There's no shame in that. Heavens, no. Each of us has to find our proper place. Take heart in the fact that you're excellent at what you do. And Brinker, Brinker, and Abbot is delighted to have you." Mr. Brinker got to his feet.

"But—"

"I have an appointment, Alison. I hope our little chat has made things clearer for you. Many young attorneys come to realize that their original goal wasn't realistic for them. The road, as you put it, that you're on is wrong for you in my judgment. No harm done. Simply pull back." He paused. "Well, I must go. I know you'll do well with Mercer Martin and the final wishes of Jeremy Daniel Boone. I'll be eager to hear your report. I'm glad you're with us, Alison."

"Thank you," she whispered.

Mr. Brinker left the room and closed the door behind him. The silence of the large expanse was oppressive, beating against Alison's mind along with all the words that Mr. Brinker had spoken to her. Her throat ached with unshed tears as she sat stiffly in the chair, knowing her trembling legs would not support her if she tried to stand.

It wasn't true, she told herself frantically. Brinker was wrong. Wrong! Granted, she hadn't scored as high as others in the mock trials in law school, but she'd been younger then, she—dear God, her dream, her goal, all she'd worked toward was to be a trial lawyer.

"Brinker is wrong," she said, getting to her feet.

She pressed her shaking fingers to her lips, hearing again Mr. Brinker's quietly spoken words. She saw in her mind's eye the understanding on his face. She knew his reputation for bringing out the best in the young attorneys he took under his wing.

Mr. Brinker was wise, Alison knew, and, indeed he did have the sixth sense he'd spoken of. All through law school she'd heard of him and his reputation for nuturing the chosen few to reach their full potential. What a party her friends had thrown for her when she'd been accepted by Brinker, Brinker, and Abbot. Friends she'd lost contact with over the months as she'd concentrated on her work.

It was just a matter of time, she'd always told herself, before Mr. Brinker gave her her first trial case, and she'd be on her way. Patience, Nick had said, and she'd waited; dreaming, seeing herself hypnotizing a jury with her presentations, her expertise.

And now, she knew, it was never going to happen.

Mr. Brinker wasn't wrong.

She had failed.

She would fall in line in the ranks of those settling for less; like her parents, like Nick, like so many others.

"Oh, God," Alison whispered, her eyes brimming with tears, "what am I going to do?"

She picked up her briefcase, lifted her chin, and left the room, praying no one would speak to her. She hardly remembered driving to her apartment, but once there, she sank onto the sofa and cried. She wept tears that seemed to rip at her soul; tears of broken dreams and shattered hopes. Never before had she felt so totally alone and lonely.

Through the hours of the evening and on into the darkness of night, Alison replayed over and over in her mind all that Mr. Brinker had said, grasping at the thought that she'd missed something, an encouraging glimmer of meaning in one sentence spoken that would mean that maybe all was not lost.

But it was hopeless, she knew deep within her, as she lay in bed staring up into the darkness. Oh, she could stay on at the prestigious firm of Brinker, Brinker and Abbot. She would be the envy of many, one of the shining stars of the community of young lawyers. But *she* would know she had failed in her goal, would never reach what she had been so sure was her full potential. She would be settling for less.

"Settling for less," Alison whispered to the night, tears choking her words. Could she ever be happy doing that? she wondered dismally. She just didn't know. She needed time to sort it all out, ease her pain, get in touch with herself. Time. And she had it, because she had given her promise to Mr. Brinker and to Tucker to follow through on the problem of Mercer Martin. It was the only case assigned to her at present, and Mr. Brinker expected her to give it her full attention and energy.

She was a temporary lawyer. She was in a temporary relationship with Tucker. Soon it would all be over. Tucker would be gone and Mercer would be with someone else in Houston. But would she have found the answer about her career?

Tucker opened one eye, groaned, then closed his eye again. "Mercer," he said groggily, "why are you standing by my bed in the middle of the night?"

"It's six in the morning, Master Boone," Mercer said. "I've brought your breakfast."

Tucker opened both eyes. "At six? In bed?"

"Well, yes, sir. Master Jeremy Boone always took his breakfast in bed at six, sir."

"Wonderful," Tucker muttered. He shoved his pillow up behind him and sat against the headboard, the sheet falling just below his waist. "Well, plunk the tray down here, I guess."

"Yes, sir," Mercer said. He hesitated a moment, then gingerly placed the tray on Tucker's thighs. "Really, sir, I never would have slept yesterday if I'd known you needed the laundry tended to."

Tucker picked up a cup and took a sip of steaming hot coffee. "What laundry?"

"That containing your pajamas, sir. I do apologize for the inconvenience you've suffered."

Tucker peered up at him. "Mercer, I don't own any pajamas."

"I'll remedy that at the first possible opportunity, sir. The kitchen is lacking in proper supplies, and I must go to market. I'll purchase your pajamas when—"

"No, no," Tucker interrupted, shaking his head. "I don't want any pajamas. I sleep nude."

Mercer's eyes widened. "In the buff, sir?"

"Naked as a jaybird."

"I see," Mercer said, staring at a spot on the far wall. "One can only hope there is never a fire requiring you to dash outside, sir."

Tucker chuckled. "It would give any nosy neighbors a real rush."

"Pardon me, sir?"

"Never mind." He took a bite of toast that was spread with jelly. "This is very good, Mercer. Thank you."

"You're quite welcome, sir."

"We'll go shopping for groceries later this morning, okay? I'll see if Alison is free to go with us."

"Very good, sir."

"You're going to be awfully hot in that suit, Mercer."

"But this is my proper attire, sir."

"Yeah, okay, whatever."

"Will there be anything else, sir?"

"No."

"When would you like me to draw your bath?"

Tucker's hand halted, a forkful of scrambled eggs halfway to his mouth, and stared at Mercer. "Draw my bath?"

"Yes, sir."

"Mercer, I don't take baths because I don't fit in bathtubs very well. I'll have my usual shower, but I can turn the faucets on all by myself. Don't give it another thought."

"If you say so, sir." He paused. "What clothes shall I lay out for you?"

"Oh, geez," Tucker said, then shoveled the forkful of eggs into his mouth.

"Sir?"

"I'll just grab a pair of jeans and a shirt. No sweat."

"No sweat? Ah, yes, sir, meaning the jeans and shirt will be clean, containing no perspiration."

Tucker sighed. "No, Mercer. 'No sweat' is a phrase that means 'no problem,' or 'nothing to worry about.' Get it?"

"Oh. Well, yes, sir, I understand, although I don't see the connection between the lack of perspiration and having no problems. Would you care for some more coffee, sir?"

"No, this is fine."

"Very good, sir. I'll return to the kitchen and prepare a list of needed supplies."

"Great idea," Tucker said quickly. " 'Bye."

"Very good, sir," Mercer said, then turned and walked from the room.

"Cheerio and all that rot," Tucker said under his breath. "Lord, I can't handle this." He reached for the telephone on the nightstand and dialed a number. The phone rang on the other end.

" 'Lo?"

"Alison? Tucker. Are you awake?"

"No," she said, and slammed down the receiver.

"Dammit," he said, then redialed the number.

Alison answered on the third ring. "What?" she yelled.

Tucker held the receiver away from his ear for a moment. "Alison, wake up. This is important."

"Nothing is important at six o'clock in the morning, Tucker. They could drop the bomb and it wouldn't be important."

"Alison, please, don't hang up."

She moaned. "Tucker, what do you want?"

You, Alison Murdock, he thought suddenly. She was in bed. He was in bed. The trouble was, they weren't in the *same* bed. "It's Mercer. It's his fault I woke you up so early. Listen, are you free to go grocery shopping? I got a few things in, but Mercer is ready to stock the place. I sure as hell hope they don't sell pajamas in grocery stores."

"What?"

"Will you go with us?"

Alison yawned. "Yes, okay. What time?"

"We'll pick you up at your place at ten. Alison, Mercer wanted to draw my bath."

She laughed. "Oh, how sweet. Do you like bubbles? Do you have a little boat or a rubber ducky to take in the tub?"

"Knock it off," he said gruffly. "He doesn't approve of me sleeping naked, either. I could tell. He really thought it was decadent. I'm sitting here in my own bed with a breakfast tray on my lap, feeling like a pervert or something because I'm nude beneath this sheet."

Nude beneath the sheet, Alison repeated slowly to herself. Tucker sat in his bed, as naked as the day he was born. Good grief, what an absolutely delicious thought. Tucker Boone in the raw. That magnificent body covered in nothing but a sheet.

"Well, he'll get used to your sleeping with your bottom bare," she said, feeling the warm flush on her cheeks. "And if you don't want him to wake you so early, just tell him. Tucker, you have crews of men working for you all over the world. You must be used to giving orders."

"But Mercer is different." Tucker dragged a hand through his tousled hair. "He's creepy. Besides, he's trying, and I don't want to be jumping all over him every two seconds."

A soft smile formed on Alison's lips. "I know, Tucker," she said quietly. "He seems so lost, confused." Just like she was. "He's going through a difficult time." Just like she was. "He needs to know that there is someone who understands what he's experiencing, someone who cares." Just as she needed that kind of someone.

"I'm trying, Alison, I really am, but I need your help."

"You have it, you know that. We agreed that we'd do this together. In fact, Mr. Brinker has given his total support to the project. I have no other cases to handle at the moment; he put the highest priority on this matter. I'm all yours, Tucker."

"Fantastic. Great. I'll see you at ten, Alison. Go back to sleep."

Alison yawned again. "I just might do that. Good-bye, Tucker."

" 'Bye," he said, then slowly replaced the receiver.

"I'm all yours, Tucker," she had said. How he liked the sound of those words. Alison—his woman, his lady. Beautiful, delicate Alison, who would nestle close to him in that big bed, sated and sleepy after their lovemaking. Lovemaking that had been slow and sweet. Passionate Alison, who would give as freely as she would take, receiving all that he was, trusting him with all that she was. They would—

"Whoa, Boone," Tucker said as heat settled low and heavy in his body. He was getting as bad as Mercer, taking words literally. "I'm all yours, Tucker." Alison had been referring to the project with Mercer, he knew that. Yet he couldn't help but wonder what it would be like to have her say those softly spoken words to him, Tucker Boone, woman to man.

Alison Murdock, Tucker mused. Where were they headed? What was really happening between them? He wanted her physically, ached with desire at the mere thought of it. But there was so much more brewing and churning within him. There were emotions of protectiveness and possessiveness. Why, he'd even had a flash of jealousy about Nick Capoletti.

When he walked through the house, Tucker realized, he pictured Alison in the rooms, laughing, talking, sharing, being with him. When he slept in this bed, it was too big, too empty, and he wanted Alison close, all through the night.

Was he falling in love with Alison Murdock?

Tucker stiffened so suddenly that the orange juice in the small glass on the tray splashed onto the remaining toast on the plate.

Love? In love with Alison? he asked himself with a surge of panic. No. Love meant being responsible for another person, making sure they were safe, happy, cared for. Safe . . . safe . . . no! He couldn't do that again, couldn't take on the burden of being certain no harm would come to someone he was directly responsible for. He couldn't because—

Tucker ran his hands down his face and drew a steadying breath. Easy, Boone, he told himself. Relax. He didn't know that he was in love with Alison. But if he *was* falling in love with her? What, then? He'd square off against it if it happened. *If*. In the meantime he was going to kiss Alison, hold her, and when the time was right, they'd make love. They would make beautiful love together. It would be like nothing he'd experienced before. He'd take her into his arms, then—

"That's all," he said gruffly as his body once again reacted to his wandering thoughts. "Go take a shower, Boone. A very *cold* shower!"

• • •

Alison peered in the mirror and decided she looked fairly normal after her shower. Cold compresses had erased the puffiness from her eyes caused by her marathon crying jag. A touch of cover-up makeup camouflaged the shadows beneath those eyes created by lack of peaceful sleep. She was dressed in a perky red blouse and white shorts, her hair was a shiny mass of fluffy, dark curls, and she'd practiced a cheerful smile until her cheeks ached.

Tucker would never know she was a total wreck. Her appearance gave no clue, she was sure, to the fact that the bottom had fallen out of her world, her road destroyed, her hopes, dreams, and goals all blown to smithereens. She was going shopping for groceries, and beyond that she refused to think.

She was being a coward, she knew it, but she didn't care. The tears were still hovering close, threatening to spill over at the slightest provocation. She couldn't, wouldn't, come apart in front of Tucker, have to explain to temporary Tucker Boone that she had failed in her career. She couldn't bear for him to know that she was less than she'd claimed to be.

No, she reaffirmed in her mind, she didn't want to fall short in Tucker's eyes. He was too important, too special, meant too much to her.

Alison blinked. Just *how* important and special was Tucker Boone to her? she asked herself. Just how much did he, his very existence, mean to her life?

Temporary . . . temporary . . . temporary.

Darn it, she thought, fuming, she had to remember that. Tucker Boone was temporary. If she did something stupid like falling in love with the man, she'd never speak to herself again.

"Do you hear me, Alison Murdock?" she said to her reflection in the mirror. "Pay attention. Whatever feelings you're having for Tucker, they do not add up to love. Got that?"

Alison spun around and marched out of her bedroom. That would really cap it, she thought, raging on, really ice the crummy cake her life had become. If she fell in love with Tucker, she could add a broken heart to her list of miserable miseries. Because love wasn't temporary, but Tucker Boone was.

A knock sounded at the door, and Alison produced one of her practiced smiles as she answered the summons. She flung the door open.

"Well, hello, Temp . . . I mean, Tucker. My, my, you look sporty." Her gaze swept over him, her heart racing. "Khaki shorts, khaki polo shirt . . . going on safari? That was a joke. I'm all ready to go to the grocery store. Where's Mercer?"

Tucker frowned. "Waiting in the car. Are you all right?"

"Me? Yes, of course, why wouldn't I be?"

"May I come in?"

"Why? I could just come out."

"Because I want to kiss you. I can kiss you out here in the hall if you like, but some of your neighbors might see us." He shrugged. "It's up to you. I *am* going to kiss you, though."

Well, Alison thought rather giddily, at least something was going right today. "Come in, Tucker," she said, stepping back.

Tucker came into the room, closed the door, pulled

Alison into his arms, and studied her face. "Are you sure you're okay? You seem . . . I don't know, tense, wired." Lord, she was beautiful. She felt so good in his arms, smelled like flowers and . . . was he falling in love with this woman?

"I'm fine."

"Not just fine," he said, lowering his head toward hers, "you're sensational. This kiss is going to be sensational."

"When?"

"Right now."

The kiss *was* sensational.

It was long and sensuous, and for Alison it was exactly what she needed to push away her gloom. She filled her senses, her very being, with the essence of Tucker. Her body hummed with the pure joy of being held in his strong arms as she answered the demands of his lips and tongue in total abandon. She melted against him, trembling with the want of him, savoring his taste and aroma. There was nothing but the moment, the kiss, and Tucker Boone.

Ah, Alison, Tucker thought hazily, drinking in her sweetness. She was so soft, so passionate, so . . . his. Now he felt complete with Alison in his embrace. He wanted her and needed her. And he knew, even as his desire consumed him, that there was a tremendous difference between the two. Was this love?

He lifted his head a fraction of an inch to draw air into his lungs.

"Tucker," Alison said, her voice unsteady, "Mercer must be getting awfully hot in the car."

He chuckled, then slowly, reluctantly, stepped back, releasing her. "I'm getting awfully hot standing here kissing you, darlin', but my problem has nothing to do with the weather."

"Ah, well"—Alison patted her curls in a fluttering gesture—"we'd better do it. The grocery shopping," she added quickly. She snatched up her purse and opened the door. "Are you ready?"

Tucker grinned at her. "To do it? Oh, yes, ma'am."

"The groceries!"

"Yeah, sure. I'm ready to shop too."

Alison rolled her eyes heavenward, then left the apartment. Tucker's gaze slid over her, missing no detail of her lissome form clad in the red cotton blouse and white shorts.

Dying, he decided, closing the door behind him. He was definitely a dying man.

Mercer greeted Alison with a polite, "Good morning, mum." No one spoke as they drove to a large supermarket. Inside the store, Mercer stood statue-still and looked around.

"Is something wrong, Mercer?" Alison asked.

"No, mum. Well, yes, mum. I'm used to shopping in a small village, going door to door for fruit, then meat, then bread."

"Oh, I see," Alison said, smiling. "Well, isn't this handy? The whole bit is under one roof."

"I say, this is quite amazing, isn't it?" Mercer said, nodding. "One hardly knows where to begin."

Tucker grabbed a cart. "I'll push, and you fill it up, Mercer. Just take your time and get what you need. We'll start with the first aisle and work our way over. What's on the top of your list there?"

"Kidneys."

"Kidneys?" Alison and Tucker said in unison.

"For kidney pie."

Tucker stepped behind Mercer where the older man couldn't see him and waved his arms frantically in the air at Alison as he mouthed, "No, no, no." Alison glared at him, then smiled at Mercer.

"Mercer," she said, "due to the ozone layer here in the United States, animals that graze in the open are extremely healthy, except for their kidneys." She sighed dramatically. "Alas, we have been forced to sacrifice the luxury of kidney pie."

"It's a damned shame," Tucker said solemnly.

"That it is, sir," Mercer said. "I planned on preparing kidney pie for supper this evening."

Tucker snapped his fingers. "Shucks. Well, we'll settle for something else. Hamburgers."

"Don't push your luck, Boone," Alison said, laughing. "I doubt seriously if Mercer has ever cooked a hamburger."

"No, mum, I haven't."

"I'll teach you," Tucker said. "Now, you tally-ho right down that aisle, Mercer, and start grabbing the stuff off the shelves."

"Very good, sir," Mercer said. "That is, no sweat." He walked away.

"Ozone layer?" Tucker said to Alison.

"It worked, didn't it?"

"And I'm eternally grateful. I had kidney pie at my grandfather's once. Alison, that was—" He shivered. "I don't want to think about it. I've definitely got to teach Mercer how to make hamburgers." He paused and frowned. "I don't know how to make hamburgers."

"For Pete's sake," Alison said, starting after Mercer, "you're as hopeless as he is."

Hopelessly in love, maybe, Tucker thought.

It was fun.

Alison wasn't sure why she was having such a good time, as there was nothing exciting, in her opinion, about grocery shopping. She did, however, have a sneaky suspicion that it had to do with the company. Tucker appeared to be as fascinated as Mercer by all the choices available in the huge store. The cart was soon filled to overflowing. Tucker put it in Mercer's care, then went and got another one. Alison trudged along merrily, offering her opinions whether they were asked for or not.

"We need snacks," Tucker said.

"I thought we might have bread and butter with sugar sprinkled on top at teatime, sir," Mercer said.

"No, Mercer, snacks. Junk food. Chips and dip, beer and pretzels," Tucker said. "Cookies and ice cream. You know, good garbage stuff."

Alison closed her eyes and shook her head. "That was the wrong thing to say."

"Good garbage, sir?" Mercer said, his eyes wide.

"Pretend he didn't say that, Mercer," Alison said. "Go back to the part about snacks. And, Mercer . . . Tucker really doesn't care for tea. Just buy enough for yourself."

"Oh, no need, mum. I can't tolerate it myself."

Tucker whooped with laughter, and the trio headed down the next aisle.

Mercer picked up a package of chocolate-chip cookies. "Would these qualify as good garbage, sir?"

"You bet," Tucker said, smiling. "Put those right in the cart, Mercer. You're really getting the hang of this."

"Thank you, sir. I must say, I'm having a rather jolly time. I'm most pleased that we're in no hurry to . . . to split. There's just so much to see. I say, look at all those jellies and jams." He hurried forward.

"Oh, Tucker," Alison said, "he's so sweet, and he's trying so hard."

"Yeah, he really is giving it his best shot. Not everyone would do that if his life suddenly went through a major upheaval. Hey, Mercer," he said, pushing the cart along, "be sure to get grape jelly."

Alison slowly followed behind. Yes, she mused, Mercer was to be commended for the effort he was making to adapt to his new life. Would she do that well? How could she know, when she wasn't even sure what the future held, what decisions she'd make? Well, she wouldn't think about any of that now. She was having too much fun with Tucker and Mercer—in a grocery store, of all places.

Having fun in a grocery store. Was this, she wondered, one of the things people did when they slowed down and smelled the flowers?

Five

Alison, Tucker, and Mercer returned to Tucker's house to find the property swarming with the work crews Tucker had hired. One group was scraping old paint off the outside of the house, another was working on the barn, and a third was tending to the weeds with heavy-duty power mowers.

Tucker helped tote in the multitude of grocery bags, then left the house to check on the jobs being done outside.

"Well, Mercer," Alison said, "let's see if we can find a home for all these goodies."

"Yes, mum."

"This is a marvelous kitchen," she said, beginning to pull food from the bags. "It's so big and cheerful. In fact, I like the whole house—not that I've seen all the rooms, of course. It's huge. My entire apartment could fit into this kitchen. Are the upstairs bedrooms nice?"

"I would say so, mum," Mercer said, neatly folding an empty bag. "Master Boone's suite is quite large, then there are two other bedrooms up there. Here, below, is my room and bath, a library, and the formal dining room, as well as the rooms you've seen. They all need a good cleaning, mum, but I'll be tending to that."

"Are all the rooms furnished?"

"Yes, mum. It wouldn't take much fuss to turn one bedroom into a nursery, though, if you pardon my saying so, mum."

Alison stopped with a can of beans in one hand and bunch of carrots in the other. "A what?"

"A nursery, mum, for the little one, the next Boone. It was Master Jeremy's wish, you see, that Master Tucker would carry on the family name here. Many an hour Master Jeremy talked about that, he did. He was very fond of Master Tucker, wanted to see him settled and happy, with a family. That was why, mum, he left this property to Master Tucker, and why he asked me to come ahead here once he was gone. Excuse me, mum, I'm not usually one to talk so much. I do beg your pardon."

"No, please don't feel that way, Mercer," Alison said. "I enjoy talking to you." She continued working, hauling a ten-pound bag of potatoes out of a sack. "You know, Mercer, not everyone is meant to settle down and raise a family. Your Master Jeremy must have been aware that Tucker traveled almost constantly."

"Certainly, mum," Mercer said, placing canned

goods on a cupboard shelf, "but Master Jeremy never believed his grandson was really and truly happy, wandering as his parents did, rest their souls."

"Have you told Tucker all this, Mercer?"

"No, mum. There's hardly been time, and I'm not sure it's my place to do so. It would seem to me, mum, that you'd be the one to tell him."

"Me? Why me?" she said, putting ice cream in the freezer.

Mercer turned to look at her. "Well, mum, it's quite obvious from the way Master Tucker conducts himself around you that he's very smitten with you. I don't expect there are any secrets between the two of you. It would be more fitting for you to tell him of Master Jeremy's hopes."

Alison opened her mouth, closed it, then emptied another grocery bag. She took a deep breath and let it out slowly.

"Mercer," she said, not looking at him, "I'm afraid you've misinterpreted what you've observed between me and Tucker. What I mean is—"

"Lunch!" Tucker roared, coming in the back door and interrupting Alison. "I'm starving. What's on the menu?"

"We'll get lunch as soon as we finish putting all this away, Tucker," Allison said.

"Great," Tucker said. He slid his hand to the nape of her neck, pulled her close, and gave her a fast, hard kiss. "That will hold me until lunch. Holler out the door when you want me to come in." He strode away and disappeared back outside.

Don't blush, Alison, she told herself firmly.

She shot a glance at Mercer, who was looking at

her with an expression of pure innocence on his face. She blushed.

"That wasn't what you thought it was, Mercer."

"Mum?" he said, raising his eyebrows slightly.

"I mean, Tucker kissed me, but . . . This is Texas, you know. People are very friendly here, a real kissin' bunch of folks. Yes, sir, they just go around—darn it, Mercer, stop looking at me like that."

"Like what, mum?"

"Like you know something I don't know. You're acting very smug. Yes, smug. Mercer, Tucker and I are not going to fill this house with little ones, understand?"

"If you say so, mum. I'd best get started on lunch. Master Boone is obviously a man of great appetite."

Alison narrowed her eyes. "What is that supposed to mean?"

"Only that I'd best prepare his lunch, mum."

"You do that," Alison said. "I believe I'll go out and have a word or two with Master Tucker Boone."

"Very good, mum. You'll inform him of Master Jeremy's final wishes?"

"You bet your patookus I will."

"Beg your pardon, mum?"

"Never mind," Alison said, then marched out the back door.

"Very, very good, mum," Mercer said pleasantly to no one.

Alison found Tucker by one of the corrals, measuring the spaces where boards were missing.

"Tucker," she said, coming up behind him.

"What?" he said, turning to look at her. "Is lunch ready?"

"No, not yet. Tucker, I need to speak to you. I just had a rather, shall we say, informative conversation with Mercer."

"Oh?"

"It seems, Master Boone, that your grandfather purposely purchased this property . . ."

Tucker laughed. "Purposely purchased this property? Can you say that really fast three times in a row?"

"Darn it, Tucker, this is serious."

"Sorry, darlin'." He took her arm. "Let's go under that tree over there and get out of the heat."

Beneath the tree, Tucker crossed his arms loosely over his chest, leaned one shoulder against the trunk of the tree, and looked at Alison.

The sun filtered through the leaves, giving the appearance, Alison thought suddenly, of golden raindrops falling over Tucker. His sun-streaked hair was thick and silky, his tan a bronzed glow, and the rugged contours of his handsome face beckoned to her to trace his features with her fingertips. The muscles in his arms strained against the sleeves of his polo shirt; the strength of his legs was evident in the khaki shorts he wore. He was like the tree: massive, strong, not needing to speak to make his powerful presence known.

Tucker was beautiful. Tucker was creating a flutter in her chest and a curl of heat in her stomach. She wanted to lift her hands to frame his face, then press her lips, and her entire body, to his; feel him, taste him, inhale his aroma. But the tree, Alison knew, would be there for an endless stretch of time. Tucker would not. Tucker was temporary.

"Alison," Tucker said, his voice low, "I'm not quite sure why you came out here, but if it has anything to do with what I'm seeing in your eyes, do remember that the place is crawling with workmen. Darlin', give me a break. You're driving me crazy looking at me like I'm the dessert you plan to have after lunch."

Alison jerked in surprise. "I was *not* looking at you like you were a dish of ice cream!"

He chuckled. "I think it would be safer to change the subject. You said you talked to Mercer?"

"Who? Oh, yes, Mercer." She cleared her throat and sent a mental directive to her body to please, *please,* calm down. "Tucker, your grandfather purposely purchased—"

He grinned at her. "Are we doing *that* again?"

"Would you stop it and just listen? It's a plan, a plot. Jeremy Daniel Boone felt you weren't really happy wandering around the world. He pictured you here, settled in with a wife, a family. That's why he left you this place and arranged to have Mercer come to help. Mercer informed me—are you ready for this—that one of the upstairs bedrooms could easily be changed into a nursery for a baby! Mercer thinks that I, that you and I . . . he really does think that. Well?"

Tucker nodded slowly. "It wouldn't be hard to turn one of those rooms into a nursery. Fresh paint, maybe wallpaper with clowns or bunnies—"

"What?" Alison shrieked. "Have you been out in the sun too long? Tucker, Mercer has to be set straight. He's not even staying here, let alone bouncing babies on his knee. He's leaving, then you're leaving—"

"I'm staying," Tucker said, looking directly into her eyes. He was? Yes, dammit, he was. He didn't even know when he'd made up his mind for certain about it, but he was staying. It felt right, good. He was home.

"What?" Alison whispered.

"I wondered if my grandfather had had a sneaky motive behind willing me this place. He did, apparently. Well, it worked. He knew me well, the old buzzard, and he loved me, Alison. He sensed what I didn't know yet, but I know it now. I want roots. It's time for me to have permanence in my life." He glanced around, then looked at her again. "I've come home, Alison, and it feels fantastic."

Oh, thank heavens, Alison thought.

No, no, no, another voice within her shouted. Tucker was supposed to be temporary. He was for now, for a snatch of stolen time, then she was to concentrate on her career.

Her career as a trial lawyer? the quiet voice asked. The one at which she'd failed?

"Alison, what's wrong?" Tucker said. "You're very pale all of a sudden. Is my staying here that upsetting to you? I'm still aware of how important your career is to you."

"That's nice," Alison said with an hysterical little giggle.

Tucker pushed himself away from the tree, took a step toward her, and circled her waist with his arms.

"But I'm also aware," he went on, "that there really is something special happening between us, and I have every intention of finding out what it is.

That's the first step, darlin'. We'll just take this one step at a time."

And where in those ever-famous steps, Alison wondered dismally, was she supposed to tell Tucker that she was a failure, someone who was going to have to settle for less than she'd planned?

"Everything is going to be fine, Alison, you'll see," Tucker said.

No, it wasn't, she thought, staring at a button on his shirt. She had to think, sort, sift through the confusion hammering in her mind. But in about two seconds she wouldn't be able to think at all, because Tucker was going to kiss her. She knew he was. She wanted him to, and that was that.

Alison lifted her head; Tucker lowered his. His mouth melted over hers, his tongue delving into her mouth. He pulled her to him, nestling her to the cradle of his hips.

Tucker was staying, Alison's mind whispered from a faraway place. Tucker was staying, and it was a frightening thought, as staggering as the one where he went away, leaving her with a broken heart should she have been foolish enough to fall in love with him.

Alison sunk her fingers into Tucker's thick hair, urging his mouth harder onto hers, trying desperately to quiet the voices in her head. She just wanted to feel, not think. Taste, not think. Savor, not think. She just wanted Tucker Boone.

Tucker's breathing was rough as he moved his seeking lips to the slender column of her throat, then claimed her mouth again. He could feel his arousal straining against the material of his khaki shorts, knew he had to stop kissing Alison before he slipped over the edge of control.

But, oh, Lord, he wanted her. Heat gathered low and heavy in his aching body, but separate and apart from his passion was a warmth, a sense of peace, that had come with speaking aloud the words that he was saying, that he'd come home.

And in the scenario in his mind that glowed with the rightness of permanence, of roots, of belonging somewhere he could call his own, he envisioned her next to him in that big house, not just in bed, but sharing all there was in this new world he hadn't known until now that he needed.

He wanted, needed, Alison to be by his side.

Because he loved her.

Lord, no! Loving meant being responsible for another, being sure they were safe from harm and—

No!

Tucker jerked his head up and looked at Alison. His heart beat wildly when he saw the tears clinging to her lashes as she slowly opened her eyes.

God help him, he thought, he loved her.

And he was scared to death.

"Why are you crying?" he asked, his voice raspy with passion.

"I'm . . . I'm very confused, Tucker," she said, trembling, "all muddled up. So much has happened so quickly. I need to be alone right now. I know I'm supposed to stay close to Mercer, but I can't, not today. Would you take me home, please?"

"Don't run, Alison. I realize this has hit us fast and hard, but we'll talk about it."

"No, it's more than just us. I really do need to be alone."

He studied her pale face for a long moment. "Yeah, okay, I'll drive you back into town. I don't like it, but I'll do it. I'll tell Mercer that the sun got to you and you're not feeling well."

"Thank you. I'll meet you at the car. Please bring my purse from the living room." She moved out of his arms. "I'm sorry. I just need time to think, sift, and sort . . . alone." She turned and started away.

He couldn't let her go, he thought frantically, not like this. She'd sort everything through, and she didn't have all the facts. Alison didn't know that . . .

"I love you," he said.

She stopped, her back to him. The air seemed to swish from her lungs, and a wave of dizziness caused her to weave unsteadily on her feet. She turned slowly to face him.

"What?" she whispered.

"I love you," he said again. "You're going home to think, about us, about your career, how it can or can't all fit together. I can't let you weigh and measure all that without telling you how I feel. I fell in love with you practically at first sight. It scares the hell out of me, but that doesn't change it. I thought you should know."

He loved her? Alison repeated silently. Tucker Boone was in love with her? Oh, damn, not now, not when she was so confused. Where was she supposed to put this? And loving her frightened him. But why?

"I . . ." she began, then threw up her hands.

"You don't have to say anything right now. Go to the car. I'll be along as soon as I tell Mercer."

Alison nodded and turned again before Tucker could see the fresh tears filling her eyes. She hurried toward the car.

Tucker drew shaking hands down his face. "Ah, man," he said. "Ah, damn, what a mess."

He walked toward the house. He was in love for the first time in his life. He was sure it was supposed to be a joyous event, a momentous occasion. Instead he had a knot of fear in his gut, and the woman he loved had tears in her eyes. Dandy. Just wonderful. Love wasn't like this in the movies. Where were the violins, the smiles of happiness, the waves crashing on the shore, or whatever the hell they had done in that movie he'd seen? Damn.

With a shake of his head Tucker entered the kitchen. "Mercer?"

"Yes, sir?" Mercer said, looking up from where he was working at the counter.

"Alison has had too much heat and isn't feeling well. I'm going to take her home."

"Yes, sir. I'm sorry madam is under the weather. I trust she'll be up to par soon?"

"I hope so," Tucker said.

"Perhaps . . . perhaps I upset Miss Alison by what I told her, sir. I'm not one to go on as I did, but it didn't seem proper my knowing Master Jeremy's final wishes when no one else did. I thought Miss Alison was the one to tell because you obviously are very smitten with her."

"Smitten?" Tucker echoed, smiling slightly. "Great word. Try this on for size: I'm in love with her."

"That's what I said, sir. However, you don't appear overly enthusiastic about it."

"Well, it sure isn't like it is in the movies, chum."

"Beg your pardon, sir?"

"Never mind. I'd better get out to the car before Alison melts from the heat."

"Very good, sir. I'll just wrap these sandwiches until you return."

"Fine. Don't worry about the work crews. They know what they're to do." Tucker started across the room, then stopped. "Sandwiches?" he said, looking back at Mercer. "Did you cut off the crusts from the bread?"

"Not yet, sir. I was just about to do that."

"Well, don't. This is Texas. We're very macho here. We eat our sandwiches with crusts. Get it?"

"Very well, sir. Even in England we know about macho. I'll certainly leave the crusts in place."

"Good. All my problems should be solved this easily. I'll see you later."

"Very good, sir. Please tell Miss Alison that I sincerely hope she'll feel better very soon." He paused. "If I might say so, sir, these things do have a way of working themselves out."

Tucker looked at Mercer for a long moment. "Do you think so?"

"There's no doubt in my mind."

"Thanks, Mercer," Tucker said, then left the room.

"No doubt in my mind at all, sir," Mercer murmured to the plate of sandwiches.

As Alison and Tucker drove back into town the

tension in the car was nearly palpable, and the silence hung heavily in the air. Alison stared straight ahead, her hands clutched tightly in her lap. Tucker glanced at her often, feeling the knot in his gut twist each time he looked at her.

At Alison's apartment building, Tucker pulled into a parking place and turned off the ignition.

"Tucker," Alison said softly, staring at her hands, "are you positive that you love me?"

He folded his arms on the top of the steering wheel and looked out the front window.

"Yes. Yes, Alison, I'm sure."

"Why did you say that loving me scares the hell out of you?"

Tucker sighed a weary sigh.

"Is it because of my career?" Alison went on. "Because I've said that nothing would keep me from staying on the road to my goal?"

"No."

"Then what—"

"Let's go upstairs to your place," he said, interrupting her. "It's too hot to sit here in the car."

"Yes, all right."

Neither spoke as they entered the building and rode up in the elevator to Alison's floor. Inside her living room, she turned to Tucker.

"Would you like something to drink?" she said.

"No."

"Would you like to sit down?"

"No."

"Tucker, I don't think this is the time to discuss anything."

"Sit down, Alison."

"No."

"Dammit, sit down!"

She plopped onto the sofa. "You don't have to yell."

"I'm sorry," he said, raking a hand roughly through his hair. "The last hour or so hasn't been the high point of my life. When a man falls in love, he doesn't expect to feel like he's just been told he has to have six root canals. This isn't going right, Alison. It's all out of whack."

"Yes, I know."

"Alison, do you love me?"

"Tucker, please don't ask me that right now. I think the answer is here, inside me, but I have to get in touch with myself to find it. I can't deal with knowing just yet. I have to get in touch with myself about other things, too, and it's too much all at once. I don't even have anywhere to file the fact that you love me. Am I thrilled? Depressed? You're in love with me, and I can't figure out how I feel about that."

"Yeah, well, love is serious business."

"Why does loving me scare the hell out of you?"

"Because it makes me responsible for you," he said, none too quietly. "Responsible for your happiness, your safety. It's up to me to keep you from harm, and I swore I'd never put myself in that position again. But, dammit, I can't stop loving you just because I'm scared spitless. So, here I am in love with you, scared out of my mind, and having no idea how you feel about me! I think I'll settle for the root canals."

"Tucker, you said *again*. Have you been in love before?"

"No. No, not the way you mean."

Alison frowned. "I don't understand."

"I didn't intend to get into this today," he said, beginning to pace the floor, "but I have to, I guess. No, I haven't been in love in the way that I love you. I've never said those words to another woman. But I have loved—my parents, my grandfather—and I was comfortable with that kind of family love. Then I went a step further, outside of that family circle."

He sat down in a chair and leaned forward, resting his elbows on his knees and clasping his hands loosely together. He stared at the far wall.

"It was in Brazil," he said, his voice suddenly flat and low. "Two years ago in Brazil. I own a small coffee plantation down there. I got word while I was in Alaska that there'd been an earthquake in the area of my property in Brazil, and I flew right down there. God, it was a nightmare."

Tucker stopped speaking and continued to stare at the wall as though a film were running, showing him in vivid detail what he'd witnessed. Alison waited, her eyes riveted on Tucker.

"So many of my people, my workers," he went on, "were dead. My manager and his wife were gone, but their eight-year-old son had lived. His name was Ricky, which was short for something I never could pronounce. Damn, he was a cute kid—big dark eyes, shaggy black hair, always into something. I'd bring him a present whenever I came, and he'd get so charged up. He followed me everywhere when I was there, never left my side. I was his hero, his mother said. He was a great kid."

"He wasn't hurt in the earthquake?" Alison said, leaning slightly forward.

"No. No, he'd been on a field trip with his class from school. They'd gone by bus and were miles away. He felt the tremors, but that's all. When the bus came back, there was nothing but destruction and death."

"Oh, Tucker."

"I got down there as quickly as I could. Ricky was in a shelter they'd put up, and I found him. He clung to me, so scared, so confused about why his parents were gone. I told him that I loved him—I did love him, Alison—and that I'd take care of him, make sure he was safe. He didn't have any relatives, no one, and I was thinking I'd adopt him or something, I don't know. All I knew was that I loved him, he was my responsibility, and I'd sworn nothing would happen to him."

Tucker stopped speaking again, and Alison felt the ache of tears in her throat as she saw the pain in his eyes.

"What happened?" she said, hardly above a whisper.

"Ricky got hysterical if I was out of his sight. I kept him with me day and night as I went about surveying the damage to the plantation, working with the officials to supply names of people who had been there at the time of the earthquake. Then one day I had to go into the city to identify some bodies. I didn't want Ricky anywhere near that. I told him to stay at the plantation with a family there, and that I'd be back before dark. He went nuts; crying, screaming, begging me not to leave him. I swore to him that he'd be safe, that I knew what was best. I had to pry him off me so that I could go. He was so damned scared."

Unnoticed tears spilled onto Alison's cheeks.

"While I"—Tucker's voice was thick with emotion—"while I was in the city there was another earthquake. I felt the tremors and I knew . . . I knew without anyone telling me . . . that Ricky was dead."

"Tucker, no!"

"He'd been waiting for me by the gate to the plantation. No one could get him to budge. When the earthquake hit, the heavy gate fell on him. I found him there . . . dead."

"I'm so sorry, Tucker," Alison said, tears still streaming down her face.

"It was my fault. I never should have left him. I'd told him I'd keep him safe, but I didn't do it. I'd loved him, I'd been responsible for him, and he was dead. I made up my mind that I'd never be responsible for anyone again, not ever. That's why finding out about Mercer blew my mind. Mercer was trusting me to look out for him in a strange, new country, and I didn't want any part of it. I'd be responsible for Mercer. I'd been responsible for Ricky."

"Tucker, it's entirely different. You must know that."

"Maybe I do, somewhere in my head, but when you told me that Mercer was coming, all I could think about was Ricky."

Tucker got to his feet and shoved his hands into his back pockets. He still didn't look at Alison.

"Then . . . you. You knocked me over, Alison. From

the first minute I saw you, I was a goner. I fell in love with you before I even knew what hit me. I love you, I don't know how to stop loving you, and I'm scared beyond belief, because I'd loved Ricky, and he's dead, and I was responsible for him because of my love, and—"

"Please, Tucker, don't," Alison said. She got to her feet and rushed across the room, wrapping her arms around his waist and leaning her head on his chest. He pulled his hands from his pockets and held her tightly to him. "Don't do this to yourself, Tucker. You've suffered enough. Ricky's death wasn't your fault." She nearly choked on a sob. "It wasn't. You did what you felt was best for him."

"He's dead!"

"Yes. An act of nature killed him. It wasn't you who did it. You've mixed it all up in your mind, twisted your beautiful love for a little boy into guilt about something that you had no control over. You've got to separate the love from the guilt, don't you see?" She lifted her head to look up at him.

"Ah, damn," he said with a groan. "I've made you cry."

"Yes, I'm crying because what you told me was sad, tragic. My heart aches for you and for Ricky. But, Tucker, please, listen to me. Your loving me doesn't make you responsible for my happiness, or my safety. If . . . if I discovered that I loved you, we would build our happiness together, equally. My safety? There are things we can't control, accidents that happen, illness. I would be responsible for myself, for making sure I didn't foolishly put myself in harm's way. That's it—that's all a person can do.

Yes, Tucker, love can be frightening, but not for the reasons you're tormenting yourself with. Let Ricky rest in peace, and put your own guilt to rest."

"But—"

"No. Tucker, I don't know what's going to happen between us. One of us, both of us, could be hurt because love sometimes comes to the wrong people at the wrong time. But it wouldn't be your fault. Do you understand?"

"I . . . maybe . . . I don't know. I've had this bottled up inside of me for two years. Hearing the words, saying it all, makes it clearer somehow. I loved Ricky. He didn't belong in that city with me that day because of what I had to do. I made that decision based on love. The earthquake was not . . . it wasn't my fault."

"No, it wasn't."

"But, Alison, if my loving you hurts you in any way . . ."

"It will simply mean that we weren't meant to be, Tucker. I don't have that answer now. I'm just too confused about too many things."

"What if I've confused you further by telling you about Ricky? What if you mix love with pity?"

"I won't. I promise you that, Tucker. I'm glad you told me, honored that you did. I know and understand you so much better now. I wish I could say to you what you want to hear. I wish I wasn't a befuddled mess, but I am. I need time to sort things through. But please believe me when I tell you that should I ever say that I love you, it will be true. I won't say those words to you unless I know in my heart and soul that it's how I feel."

"I believe you." He lifted his hands and wove his fingers through her silken curls. "And I love you. I won't give you up without a fight, Alison. I've waited a lifetime for you without realizing what was missing from my existence. You'll have all the time you need to sort and sift, but I'll be close by." He lowered his head toward hers. "Very close."

As Tucker's mouth covered hers, Alison felt a shudder rip through him and knew what it had cost him to bare his soul and tell her the painful story of losing Ricky. Tucker had been vulnerable before her, had relived the horror of it all so that she could understand him better, know the fears and doubts that accompanied his love for her. What an incredible man Tucker Boone was!

Alison leaned farther into him, wishing to warm and soothe him, erase the memories that haunted him. She met his tongue with her own and heard a groan rumble deep in his chest.

Tucker dropped his hands to Alison's back and pulled her close, feeling her breasts press against him. Blood pounded in his veins as the kiss became hungry, rough, his mind and body wanting more. He felt strange, disoriented, as though by telling Alison about Ricky he had stripped away all his defenses. Now he stood naked and weak in her arms. He had declared his love for her, then poured out his guts, his deepest, crippling secret regarding Ricky. And, dammit, all she'd given him in return were words, pretty platitudes that were tumbling through his mind in a jumbled maze.

Tucker tore his mouth from Alison's, lifted her into his arms, and carried her to the sofa. He laid her down, then followed her, catching the majority of his weight on his forearms as he covered her body with his.

"Tucker, what—"

"Shut up," he said gruffly, then brought his mouth down hard onto hers.

A flash of panic caused Alison to stiffen beneath him, but as Tucker's tongue plummeted into her mouth, all fear vanished. Heated desire consumed her, and she wrapped her arms tightly around his neck. She could feel his arousal heavy against her and rejoiced in knowing he wanted her as much as she wanted him. This was the time, this was the moment. They would be one.

Tucker shifted enough to unbutton her blouse, then pull it free of her shorts. His smoldering gaze swept over her breasts, covered in a lacy bra. He slid his tongue across the soft flesh of one breast, pushing above the bra as he splayed his hand flat on Alison's stomach. She purred in pleasure, her eyes drifting closed. His fingers inched beneath the waistband of her shorts, his thumb expertly flicking the front button open in the process.

While his tongue continued to tease and tantalize her breasts, he slid the zipper of her shorts down, his fingers coming to rest at the top of her bikini panties. He moved to take her mouth again as Alison lifted her hips to meet the increasing pressure of his hand. His fingers crept beneath the lace of her panties to the soft nest that covered her womanhood.

A red haze of passion crowded Tucker's mind, obscuring his sense of reality and reason. He wanted.

He needed. He ached. He would have Alison Murdock. She was his, he loved her.

A soft sob whispered from Alison's lips and cut through the fog in Tucker's brain like the sharp blade of a knife. Every muscle in his body tensed, coiled to the point of pain. He shook his head as though coming out of a trance.

"Dear Lord," he said hoarsely, "what am I doing?"

In one smooth motion he leveled himself off Alison and sat on the end of the sofa by her feet. He rested his elbows on his knees, covered his face with his hands, and took several deep, ragged breaths of air into his lungs.

Alison blinked, then struggled to sit up, her entire body trembling with desire. She clutched her blouse closed over her breasts, and drew her knees up as she stared at Tucker with wide eyes.

"Tucker," she said, her voice unsteady, "why—"

He snapped his head around to look at her, his eyes flashing with an emotion Alison couldn't decipher.

"I don't know why," he said, his voice raspy. "Dammit, I'm sorry. Something happened. I felt . . . I don't know. I've never forced myself on a woman before. Not ever." He laughed, a sharp, bitter sound. "And I claim to love you? Right." He shook his head. "Ah, damn, I'm sorry. I don't know what else to say, and I know it's not good enough."

"Why," Alison whispered, "did you stop?"

Tucker narrowed his eyes, confusion evident on his face. "What?"

"I wanted you, Tucker," she said, her voice still hushed. "I've never wanted anyone the way I do you."

"Alison, for God's sake," he said, his voice rising, "I didn't give you a chance to think. This"—he waved his arm in the air—"was seduction, lady, running roughshod over your sense of right and wrong."

"No, it wasn't," she said, shaking her head.

"Ah, hell," he said, staring up at the ceiling for a long moment.

"I once heard that a woman must feel loved to make love, and a man must make love to feel loved."

Tucker looked at her again.

"I know you love me," she went on. "I felt loved. And you? Oh, Tucker, don't you think I know how difficult it was for you to tell me about Ricky? How hard it must be for you to continually declare your love for me and not hear those words in return? You stripped yourself bare for me, and I cherish that. I don't know if I'm *in* love with you, but I would have *made* love with you, and I wouldn't have been sorry. You needed to make love to feel loved, to receive for all you'd given me. I understand that. It wouldn't have been wrong, not for me."

Tucker continued to stare at her, and Alison lifted her chin, meeting his unwavering gaze steadily. Seconds ticked by into silent minutes.

"When Boones love," he finally said quietly, "they choose well. You're a helluva woman, Alison Murdock."

She smiled at him warmly. "And you're a helluva man, Tucker Boone."

Their eyes held for another long moment, one of greater understanding, of having faced a crisis and seen it through to its proper end, together. Then Tucker got to his feet, moved to where Alison sat, and brushed his lips over hers.

"I'll call you tomorrow," he said. "I love you and I thank you."

Tucker left the apartment, but Alison didn't move. She rested her forehead on her drawn-up knees, refused to dwell on the troubles that plagued her, and centered her mind on thoughts of Tucker. Beautiful, magnificent, complicated Tucker Boone.

Late that night, unable to sleep, Tucker pulled on his jeans and moved quietly through the house to the yard beyond the kitchen. The sky was a silver umbrella of stars, and he gazed up at them, filling his lungs with the fresh summer air.

"Good-bye, Ricky," he said, his throat tight and achy. "Rest well." Tears shimmered in Tucker's eyes. "And, Ricky? You really were a great little kid."

Six

At six o'clock the next morning Alison groaned as the telephone rang on the nightstand next to her bed. She opened one eye, willed the offensive device to shut up, and closed her eye again. The shrill ring sounded again.

"Darn it, Tucker Boone," Alison mumbled, "I'm going to strangle you." She snatched up the receiver. "Tucker, if you don't want Mercer to wake you so early, tell him, just tell him. But, for Pete's sake, don't wake *me* up to moan about it."

"Alison?"

She shot up to a sitting position, her eyes wide. That, she thought wildly, was not the voice of Tucker Boone. "Yes?" she said tentatively.

"This is Mr. Brinker."

"Oh, good Lord," Alison whispered, covering her

eyes with her hand. She dropped her hand and shook her head as she rolled her eyes heavenward.

"I'm sorry I woke you," Mr. Brinker said.

"Oh, no problem," she said breezily. "I adore mornings. They're so uniquely . . . early, or whatever."

Mr. Brinker chuckled. "I take it that Mercer Martin is used to rising with the chickens."

"We're working on that," Alison said. "We've already solved the kidney pie problem. Things are progressing nicely. I think. Maybe."

"I'm sure you'll handle it all very smoothly, Alison."

Oh, right, she thought dryly. "I'm doing my best, Mr. Brinker," she said ever so sweetly.

"Good. Alison, the reason that I'm calling you so early is that we're in a bit of a rush at the office. We've been given a new case to handle, one that I'm taking charge of myself. You'll no doubt read about it in the morning papers."

"Oh?" Alison said, now very wide-awake.

"One of our leading citizens, Mr. Vincent Munetti, has been arrested for land fraud. The charges state that he bought a great deal of property under various names at extremely low prices. He then resold the land at two and three times what he paid for it."

Alison frowned. "That sounds like a smart businessman to me."

"Not when the charges also state that he bribed a member of the city council to obtain the information that a huge shopping center was to be built on that land. He was in possession of the property by then and was able to demand and get the high resale price. The man on the city council has disappeared. I'm representing Mr. Munetti."

"I see. Well, just what is it that you want me to do?"

"I've already spoken to Nick Capoletti this morning. He wakes up about as cheerfully as you do. I gave Nick a list of items I need information on. I'd like you to meet him at the law library at eight and work with him on the research."

A painful knot tightened in Alison's stomach.

"What you'll be obtaining for me will be vitally important, Alison. The prosecutor's key witness has disappeared. I need the history of similar cases involving land purchased and sold under these types of circumstances, precedents set in a court of law in the past."

"Yes, of course," Alison said, her voice flat.

"Mr. Boone will understand that you're needed elsewhere for a few days. Assure him you'll return to the problem of Mercer Martin as quickly as possible. I must go—there's a great deal to be done. Thank you, Alison. Good-bye."

"Good-bye, Mr. Brinker," she said, then slowly replaced the receiver. Mr. Brinker was assigning legal research to her. Fine. But he wasn't giving her a co-counsel role in the case. Did he think of her as being on Nick's level? Just a paralegal? If so, it would be the last straw, the final blow to her pride, the—

The telephone rang again.

Alison glared at it. What now? she wondered. Had Mr. Brinker forgotten to tell her that she was in charge of sharpening the pencils while she worked with Nick?

She sighed and picked up the receiver. "Yes?"

"Alison? Tucker. Sorry I woke you."

"You didn't."

"Why not. Couldn't you sleep?"

Alison squeezed the bridge of her nose and closed her eyes. "What is it, Tucker?"

"Oh. Listen, I have an emergency at one of my mines in South America. Nothing dangerous or anything. Bureaucratic snafus with lost permits. My manager down there feels that the mine will be shut down for quite a while unless I get there to cut through the red tape at a higher governmental level than he's able to reach. I should only be gone a few days."

"I see," Alison said. She was going to miss him. She knew that already. She was definitely going to miss Tucker. "What about Mercer?"

"That's where you come in. I thought you could stay out here and continue to coach him while I'm gone. I hate to leave him all alone right after he's arrived. That seems like a rotten thing to do."

"Yes, it does. But, Tucker, I'm going to be tied up for a few days myself. Mr. Brinker just called me. When you read the paper, you'll see that Vincent Munetti has been arrested. Mr. Brinker is representing him, and there are things I have to do to help with the case."

"Whew. The big time, huh?"

Not quite, Alison thought glumly. Not even close.

"Alison? Are you there?"

"What? Oh, yes, I'm here."

"Look, this still can work. Could you stay out here at night? That will give Mercer excellent practice at serving the needs of a career woman. He'll have your dinner ready, fix your breakfast in the morning. That's a lot different than taking care of my grandfather in that old castle. It'll be great training for Mercer."

"Tucker, since you've decided to stay on there, and after our . . . well, our talk about Ricky, have you given any thought to letting Mercer live with you? You wouldn't be responsible for him in the way you originally pictured it."

"I don't know, Alison. I have to take this all very slowly. In the meantime I feel the best thing to do is to continue to prepare Mercer to live somewhere else. Even if I do decide to have him stay on here, he has to make a lot of adjustments to Texas living. You know what I mean?"

"I guess so. No, I don't know. Like what?"

"Like what? Well . . . his clothes, for one thing. He's going to pass out from the heat in that three-piece suit of his. And then there's the learning of some good old American slang, the cooking of hamburgers, driving on the right side of the road, and—"

"Okay, I get the point."

"Will you stay out here while I'm gone? You wouldn't want Mercer to be lonely, would you? No, of course you wouldn't. What do you say?"

"Yes, all right."

"Great. I've got to go. I'm catching a plane in a little over an hour. I'll get back as soon as I can. Thank you, Alison. I love you. 'Bye."

"Good-bye, Tucker," Alison said to the dial tone. She replaced the receiver, then slid down in the bed to stare up at the ceiling.

No, she mused, she didn't want Mercer to be lonely.

But she didn't want herself to be lonely, either. And she would be, without Tucker. What an intricate part of her life he'd become so very quickly. From the moment she'd seen him sleeping in that hammock, her world had changed.

If only, *only*, she mentally went on, her career hadn't fallen apart at the same time. Tucker Boone was enough to deal with! "In the meantime," she said sullenly, throwing back the blankets, "I'll go play paralegal with Nick Capoletti."

After saying good-bye to Alison, Tucker hung up the receiver of the kitchen telephone and turned to look at Mercer.

"Well, sir?" Mercer said.

"She bought it."

"Miss Alison purchased something, sir?"

"No, no, she believed my story, thinks I have to go away for a few days."

"Oh, very good, sir. That will give her the time she feels she needs to think."

"Right," Tucker said, pouring coffee into a mug. "But I want her out here, in this house, while she's thinking. Mercer, I've told you that I want you to stay on here, but Alison mustn't know that yet. It would complete her job for Brinker and she'd be assigned to some other case. You heard what I said to her. She believes I'm still on the fence about you going to live somewhere else."

"A touch dishonest, Master Boone."

"Desperate men to desperate things, Mercer," Tucker said, sitting down at the table. "I'm fighting a big foe—Alison's career, her dream. I've got nothing against her being a lawyer, but she sure as hell can be my wife at the same time. Trick is to get her to realize that." He frowned and took a sip of coffee. "It would help if she figured out that she loves me too. She *does* love me, dammit. She's afraid to get in touch with herself about it because her career has always come first."

"I understand, sir."

"Alison has to work on an important case for a few days. She'll stay out here at night, though. Actually this is good. She'll be here in my home, get comfortable with it, and see that because you're here, she's not facing tons of housework and cooking at the end of her day. She can marry me and still be a hotshot attorney."

"But she doesn't know I'm staying on here, sir."

"That can't be helped. She thinks *you* think you're staying, because we decided not to tell you I was thinking about you not staying. You won't have to act out much of a role. You're learning to be a Texas butler for me. Pure and simple. Okay, next problem. Where in the hell am I going to hide for the next few days? Nothing I own needs my personal attention." He shrugged. "I guess I'll go to Vegas and play poker in the casino of which I'm part owner. Yeah, that's fine. I won't be very far away. I should kidnap Alison, take her with me to Vegas, and marry her."

"I don't believe that idea has much merit, sir."

"No, I suppose not," Tucker said with a sigh. "Lord, being in love is complicated." He got to his feet. "I'll go pack."

"I would gladly pack for you, sir."

"No, I'll do it. Alison will be out here after work, Mercer. Take good care of her for me."

"Indeed I will. You're not to worry about Miss Alison while I'm looking after her."

"Thanks, Mercer."

"She's a lovely young woman, sir. Master Jeremy would be pleased."

"And I'd be pleased if I knew that Alison would agree to marry me."

"It's in the pouch, sir. I'm sure of it."

Tucker frowned in confusion. "In the what?"

"I was watching the telly in my room last night. When something is positively certain to happen, one says that it's in the pouch."

Tucker laughed. "In the *bag*."

Mercer frowned. "Oh, dear me."

"You keep watching the . . . telly. That's a great source for you. I should have thought of that myself." Tucker started toward the door. "I'd better hit the road," he said, leaving the room.

"Hit the road?" Mercer muttered to the empty room.

As Alison walked up the steps of the law library Nick pushed himself away from the wall he'd been leaning against. She frowned as she stopped in front of him.

"Nick, what's wrong?" she said. "You don't look well. Are you sick?"

"Let's go for a cup of coffee. I really need to talk to you."

"Yes, all right. You should be home in bed, though, if you're sick."

"I'm not sick, Alison, not the way you mean. Come on. There's a café down the block."

As they walked, Alison glanced often at Nick, seeing the fatigue etched on his handsome face, the tight set to his jaw. His thick black hair was tousled, as though he'd raked restless fingers through it. Nick didn't speak, and Alison waited anxiously as they entered the café and slid into a booth. It wasn't until their coffee was set in front of them that Nick sighed and met Alison's gaze.

"When Brinker called me this morning," he said quietly, "I nearly told him on the phone that I was quitting."

"Quitting?" Alison said, leaning toward him. "Why?"

Nick raised one hand to silence her. "Just listen a minute, okay?"

"Yes, I'm sorry."

"I would have quit right then, but he told me to meet you at the library and that you'd help me with the research. I knew you had to be upset. I thought about giving Brinker my opinion on that, too, but I kept my mouth zipped. I didn't want to stick you with having to do all the research, so I came over and waited for you. I'll help you locate the cases Brinker needs, but then I'm leaving the firm."

"I have to ask again, Nick," Alison said, shaking her head. "Why?"

"Vincent Munetti is my uncle."

Alison gasped.

"Cute, huh? Alison, I know you've never understood why I didn't pursue a career equal to my potential. Well, let me tell you a little story. I was a really good football player in high school. Colleges were sniffing around with scholarship offers, but then they took a hard look at my family, and one by one they pulled back. Oh, I went to college, but not on scholarship, because no one wanted to be that closely linked to me."

"I don't understand, Nick."

"I come from a very big, very powerful family, Alison." Nick drew a shuddering breath. "A very crooked family."

"No, that can't be true."

"It's true, all right. I've tried so damn hard to keep a low profile, to find a place, do my job, and not draw attention to myself. While I was in college I did some volunteer work at a medical clinic for poor people. One night some junkies broke in and stole drugs. The police investigated, and lo and behold, there was a Capoletti working there. I went through hell proving I had nothing to do with the robbery. I could give you a dozen similar examples of how I'm guilty by association . . . always. I gave up trying to go after any dreams I might have had. I just wanted some peace in my life."

"Nick, this is so unfair. How can you be blamed for what your relatives do?"

"That's the shakes and the breaks, kid," he said, a weary tone to his voice. "And now? I've had a couple of good years at Brinker, Brinker, and Abbot. I liked what I was doing, or at least I could settle for it, have my hand in, be close to the workings of the law, which I'd always loved. But sweet old Uncle Vince cooked that goose. He's as guilty as sin, Alison."

"Are you sure?" she whispered.

"Hell, yes. The missing witness? He's been paid off. The joker is soaking up the sun in Bermuda right now. My father told me the whole story last night. And me, being the dutiful son, will keep my mouth shut. I stay in Houston for my mother's sake. She's surrounded by corruption, and I'm all she has to keep her sane."

Alison covered his hand with hers on the top of the table. "I don't know what to say to you."

"There's nothing you *can* say. I have to leave Brinker, Brinker, and Abbot. This trial is big news and will stretch on for months. The yellow journalists will look for anything they can find to spice it up. They'll discover that Vincent Munetti's nephew is a paralegal at Brinker, and there will be a story on me. So much for my low profile. I'm getting out before that can happen."

"Where will you go? What will you do? Oh, Nick, I hate this."

"I'm not thrilled out of my socks, either," he said, attempting a smile that failed. "I'm thirty years old and on the run. I haven't done a damn thing wrong except having been born into the wrong family. Why do you think I mess around with so many women? I can't form a permanent attachment, fall in love, have a wife and kids. What am I supposed to say to a woman? 'Sweetheart, I'd like you to meet my family, the Crooks'? Not a chance. I want a wife, Alison, and children, but . . ." He shook his head.

"There's got to be something we can do, Nick. There has to be a way."

"Dammit," he said, pulling his hand free of hers, "quit living in a dream world, Alison. You've made up your mind how everyone's life should be—your parents, mine, *and* yours. Then you shake your head and cluck your tongue when people don't live up to your idea of what they should be. Well, I can't, because I'll never have the chance. Your parents won't, because that was the choice they made. And you? Alison, for God's sake, wake up and smell the coffee. You're never going to be a trial lawyer. But so what? I'd give anything just to have the career you can have."

"You know?" she said, her eyes wide. "You know I'm not going to be a trial lawyer?"

"I work very closely with you, Alison," he said, his tone gentling. "I figured it out. Did Brinker tell you?"

"Yes," she said, staring into her coffee cup. "Yes, he did. I feel as though I'm a failure. I had it all planned—my road was so clear in my mind."

"Ah, Alison, we don't always get what we want, and it's not necessarily our fault. You have a lot to offer people in the area of law, and it's there for you for the taking. Me? I've got a case of the shorts. I'm coming up empty-handed again."

Alison looked up at him. "Oh, Nick, forgive me. I'm sitting here feeling sorry for myself while your whole world is crashing in on you. Tell me what I can do to help you. There has to be something."

"No," he said quietly, "there isn't. I think I'm going to have to sit my mother down and try, somehow, to make her understand that I have to leave Houston. I can't live the rest of my life like this. Alison, I wanted you to know what was going on because I care about you. You're one of my few real friends. Promise me that you'll be happy." He snorted in disgust. "What a dumb thing to say. Let me rephrase that. I was trying to say, count the blessings you have in your grasp. Don't beat yourself up over what you didn't get."

"You're so dear to be thinking about me at a time like this. I do understand what you're saying to me. Thank you for being my friend, Nick. Will you keep in touch with me when you leave the firm? Please? Don't just disappear on me, I couldn't stand that."

"Yeah, I'll keep in touch."

"Nick, listen. Tucker Boone has all kinds of companies, businesses, all over the world. I could talk to him, ask him if there's a place for you somewhere."

"I'm sure he'd be ecstatic to have a guy with mob connections working for him."

"Stop it! Tucker wouldn't judge you by your family. He isn't like that. He's warm and wonderful, and he really cares about people and— Why are you smiling?"

"Why are your eyes sparkling? Why is there a blush on your cheeks, Miss Murdock?" he said, his smile growing bigger. "Do I detect a bit more going on between you and Tucker Boone than the usual lawyer-client relationship?"

She cleared her throat and glared at him. "We were discussing the possibility of your working for Tucker, Mr. Capoletti."

Nick's smile slowly faded. "Don't put Tucker Boone on the spot, Alison. If there *is* something happening between you two—which I'd bet my last ten bucks on—don't muddy the waters with your shady friend."

"But—"

"Enough of this. I'm getting thoroughly depressed.

Ever spent the day with a depressed Italian? We're talking about one sullen dude, a real piece of work. Come on, let's go research our little hearts out for good old Brinker, Brinker, and Abbot. Lord, what a bunch of hoopla for nothing. Uncle Vince will walk away from this. There's no witness, remember? Vince will be free as a bird."

"But *you* won't," Alison said softly.

"No," Nick said with a sigh. "Maybe someday I'll—Forget it. Let's go, Miss Legal Eagle. Time is a-wastin'."

Alison dropped a bill onto the table and slid out of the booth. She hugged him. "I'm so sorry, Nick."

"Me, too, kid," he said, giving her a tight squeeze.

They left the café and walked slowly back to the law library, each lost in thought.

At three o'clock that afternoon Alison closed a heavy book and smacked it with her hand. "That's it, the last of the cases that showed up on the central computer. Mr. Brinker seemed to think it would take several days to collect all this, but we can't manufacture something that just isn't there."

Nick stretched and yawned. "Amen to that. I'm out on my feet. I didn't get any sleep last night."

"Oh, darn, Nick, I don't want to be finished here. That will mean you're going to tell Mr. Brinker you're quitting, and I won't see you again."

"Sure you will," he said, smiling at her. "I'll be around, here and there—for a while, anyway." He reached over and wrote on her pad of paper. "That's the phone number at my apartment."

"Promise me you won't leave Houston without telling me. Besides, I want to talk to Tucker about you, about maybe finding a job for you. He's out of town for a few days right now, though."

Nick shook his head and got to his feet. "Don't bug Tucker Boone about me, Alison. Some guys aren't into their ladies being concerned about another man's problems."

"I'm not his lady," Alison said, rising and picking up the big book. "Well, I sort of am, but not exactly."

Nick laughed and took the book from her hands. "I'll put this away while you figure out where you stand with Tucker."

"He loves me," Alison blurted out.

"Shh," someone said in the distance. "This is a library."

"I'll be damned," Nick said, his voice hushed. "He does? That's terrific, Alison. No, it isn't, you're frowning. Why isn't it terrific?"

"Because I can't figure out how I feel about *him*, Nick. I had my life all mapped out, you know that. Then Mr. Brinker told me I would never be a trial lawyer, and I was devastated. I feel like a failure. I have to decide if I'm willing to settle for less, which I always swore I would never do. In the middle of all that, up pops Tucker. He makes me feel— I've never been so, that is, he's . . ."

"I get the message," Nick said, chuckling.

"The thing is, Nick, it's all jumbled up—Tucker, my career, everything."

Nick nodded slowly. "Yeah, I see. You're afraid you might turn to Tucker to make up for your disappointment about your career goals. What does he say about that?"

"I haven't told him that my career is in a mess."

"Why the hell not?"

"Quiet, people!" someone said.

"I haven't had the courage to tell him that I'm not up to a first-rate performance in my chosen field, Nick. I can hardly deal with it myself, let alone tell Tucker. He thinks I'm playing a very important role in this case right now. What a joke. *I'm* a joke. All I'm cut out to do is settle custody battles over tulip bulbs."

"Wrong," Nick said. He crossed the room, put the book away, and strode back to Alison. "Now, you listen to me. You're a people person. You care deeply about those you're trying to help, and you're great on a one-to-one basis. Sure, you've been given garbage cases at Brinker, Brinker, and Abbot, because garbage-case people can afford to go there. But what about the legal-aid folks? The mother trying to get child support from a bum of a father? The woman suffering sexual harassment on the job but is too afraid to speak up? The family just getting by, who has a landlord who won't fix the plumbing?"

"Legal aid?"

"You wouldn't make big bucks, but those people need help. They need someone who cares, who sees them as being just as important as those who can afford to hire a lawyer to hassle over tulip bulbs. Think about it. And, Alison? Tell Tucker Boone that you made a mistake when you set your career goals. The man has a right to know who you really are."

"I'm not sure who I really am," she said, throwing up her hands.

"Then introduce yourself to yourself, lady," a disgusted voice said, "but do it quietly."

"Oh, for Pete's sake," Alison said. "Let's get out of here."

Outside, they walked down the stairs, then stopped.

"I'll take this stuff to Brinker," Nick said, "and tell him that I'm quitting."

"Oh, Nick, I wish—"

"I'll be fine—don't worry. And I promise I won't leave Houston without letting you know."

"I'm going to cry."

"Don't! Italian men are unhinged by the sight of tears." He kissed her on the forehead. "I'll talk to you soon. Think about what I said, Alison, all of it. There's a wonderful place for you in law if you want it. In the meantime tell Tucker the truth. 'Bye, kid."

"Good-bye, Nick. I'll miss you."

"See ya," he said, then turned and went down the sidewalk.

Alison watched him go as she blinked back her tears, then she went in the opposite direction toward her car. She'd packed a small suitcase that morning, and was ready to stay at Tucker's place.

What had happened to Nick wasn't fair, she thought dismally as she drove. It was rotten and awful. She had to talk to Tucker about helping Nick find another job. And she had to tell Tucker that she'd fallen flat on her nose halfway down her road to her career goal. And she had to tell Tucker that she loved him. And she had to convince Tucker to let dear, sweet Mercer stay on, and . . .

"Pardon me?" she said to her reflection in the rearview mirror. "Could we back up a bit here?"

She had to tell Tucker that she loved him? her mind echoed. Loved him? Was she actually in love, truly and irrevocably in love with him?

"Yes!" she said as she maneuvered through the heavy traffic. "Yes, yes, yes." A lovely smile lit up her face.

Three seconds later it was replaced by a frown. "No, no, no," she mumbled. She could not, would not, tell Tucker of her love for him until her career was straightened out. If *she* had been confused by the timing of it all, what was to keep Tucker from doubting her sincerity, from squinting his eyes and wondering if she'd settled for him because of a crisis in her career?

She'd wait to tell him of her love, she decided firmly, until she had herself all squared away. That was definitely the best thing to do. Stay at Brinker, Brinker, and Abbot? Maybe. Work for legal aid? Maybe. Open a small office of her own? Maybe. But until she knew exactly who she was and where she was headed, she'd keep her declaration of love to herself. She would come to him as the self-assured woman he deserved.

When Alison pulled into the driveway at Tucker's, Mercer immediately came out of the front door. She left the car and hurried across the now neatly trimmed lawn.

"Mercer?" she said, meeting him on the porch. "What's wrong? Has something happened to Tucker?"

"Oh, no, madam, Master Boone is fine, I'm sure. It's the beasts."

"Beasts?"

"A huge truck arrived a short time ago and put

the beasts in the enclosed meadow beyond the barn. Master Boone didn't say a word about any beasts being delivered, and I hardly knew what to do. So I signed for the hideous creatures, and they're out there, a dozen of them."

"Beasts?" Alison asked slowly. "In the meadow behind the barn?"

"Yes, madam."

"Well, let's stop in the house to drop off my things, then we'll go check out those beasts."

"Oh, no, Miss Alison, I really don't believe you should go near them. I gave my solemn word to Master Boone that I would look after you while he was away. The beasts are dangerous, I'm positive of that. They're making strange noises and they have an . . . an odor, mum. They're enormous, with tails that swish, and they really do . . . smell."

"I see," Alison said, opening the door and entering the house. Mercer was right behind her. "It sounds to me, Mercer, that Tucker has had some cattle delivered to graze on that plush grass out there."

"Cattle, mum? Oh, dear me, I thought they were extinct in this country, like the buffalo."

"Mercer," she said, patting his arm, "I think you were a tad out of touch with things while you lived in that castle with Jeremy Boone. I'll go change my clothes, then we'll look at the beasts."

"Are you sure, mum?"

"Don't worry about a thing." She started toward the stairs. "Does it matter what room I use?"

"Oh, no, mum. I cleaned them all today and put fresh linens on the beds."

"Thank you."

Upstairs, Alison entered the first room she came to and found a lovely decor with a western flair and vibrant colors. A bathroom was to be shared with another bedroom beyond it. She changed quickly into shorts, a knit top, and tennis shoes. Back out in the hall, she glanced at the closed double doors at the end of the corridor.

"Tucker's room," she whispered. Tucker's bed. But no Tucker.

She ran down the stairs to find that Mercer hadn't moved from the spot where she'd left him.

"Ready?" she said.

"Really, mum, I don't think you should go out there. The work crews are gone for the day, and heaven knows I'm no match for those beasts. It's my duty to watch over you. I promised Master Boone that I would."

"I won't go too close, Mercer. Besides, that meadow is fenced in. Nothing is going to happen to me. You can stay here if you like."

"I couldn't possibly do that."

"Well, okay, let's go."

Outside, Alison marched along, trying to keep up with Mercer. They went beyond the barn to the fence surrounding the meadow.

"Cattle," Alison said with a sweep of her arm. "Good old beef on the hoof. Potential hamburgers."

"Beasts," Mercer said.

"Well, they're not pretty, but they're useful. Don't give them another thought, Mercer. Pretend they're not here."

"That's difficult to do, mum, when they have such a peculiar odor."

"You'll get used to it."

"But, mum?"

"Yes?"

"What am I supposed to feed these creatures for supper?"

Alison laughed. "Oh, Mercer, I adore you. You're wonderful. They'll eat that grass, and you won't have to fuss with them at all."

"Oh. Well, I suppose it's just no sweat, then, is it?"

"Absolutely," Alison said, nodding. "No sweat at all."

"Jolly good," he said decisively. "I do apologize for becoming so unpasted, madam."

"Unpasted?" She paused. "You mean unglued?"

"Yes, mum. They said that on the telly. There was a story, but they didn't seem to reach a satisfactory conclusion."

"I think you watched a soap opera, Mercer. You have to tune in tomorrow to see what happens next. I take it that Jeremy Boone didn't have a . . . telly?"

"Oh, no, mum. He didn't care for modern appliances and such. A soap opera. Why do they call it that?"

"I believe it's because soap companies used to be the sole sponsors of those shows back in the days of radio," Alison said, starting back toward the house. Mercer fell in step beside her. "And 'opera' certainly is appropriate, since the stories are so melodramatic."

"Quite. Those characters were terribly upset. A man said to a crying woman, 'Natalie, don't come unpasted.' "

"Unglued."

He sighed. "I do have so much to learn."

"You're doing beautifully, Mercer, and Tucker and I are going to continue to help you."

"Thank you, mum. At least one thing is said the same here in America as it is in England."

"Oh?" Alison said, swatting at a fly. "What's that?"

"The special words between a man and a woman. The words, 'I love you and I want to marry you.' "

Alison linked her arm through Mercer's as they continued to walk. "Yes," she said softly, "you're right about that. And I intend to say those words to only one man in my entire life." Only to Tucker Boone.

"Very good, mum," Mercer said. "Very, very good."

Seven

"Well, Tuck, what's the verdict?"

Tucker stood in the plush, executive offices of the Las Vegas casino and stared out the window at the city below that never slept. It was mid-afternoon, and traffic was heavy in the streets, as well as on the sidewalks. At three in the afternoon or three in the morning, it looked the same.

He'd been there a little over twenty-four hours, and he'd missed Alison with increasing intensity as each hour had ticked by. He'd hardly slept the night before, picturing Alison in his home in Houston, hearing her laughter, actually filling his senses with her aroma.

Was Alison thinking about him, them, their future together? he wondered. Was she doing her famous sifting and sorting, weighing his love for her against the demands of her career? Had she looked deep within herself and discovered her love for him? Would she embrace it, rejoice in it, declare it out loud to him when he returned home? Ah, damn, this being away from her was driving him crazy.

"Tuck? Hey, buddy, are you off on another planet or something?"

Tucker turned with a start and looked at the handsome, well-built, silver-haired man sitting behind the desk.

"Sorry, Jared. I figured this was your nap time. I know how it is with you older folks. You need your little snatches of sleep to keep you going."

Jared chuckled and shook his head. "You never lighten up on the old-man stuff. You know, and I know, that my hair was this color by the time I was twenty, just like my daddy and my granddaddy before him." There was a faint hint of a Southern accent in his voice. "We also know I'm thirty-six years old, flake brain."

"And," Tucker said, grinning at him, "we know that the women swoon at the sight of your body, that intriguing hair of yours, and your big baby blues."

"Yeah, well, what can I say?" Jared sighed dramatically. "The kid here has the stuff that it takes. Of course, you're no slouch in that department, either, Boone. I've noticed, however, that you're not looking back at what's looking at you this trip."

"Not interested," Tucker said gruffly.

Jared hooted with laughter and smacked the desk with the palm of his hand. "The man has gone and done it. Not interested, he says? Put that together with the lost-puppy-look on your face and it all adds up. You're down for the count. You're in love!"

"Knock it off," Tucker said, beginning to pace the floor. "I never said that I was in love."

"What's her name?"

"Alison," Tucker said, before he'd realized he'd said it.

Jared roared with laughter again.

Tucker stopped in front of the desk, planted his hands flat on top, and leaned forward. "Can it, Jared. Cork it right now."

"Yes, suh," Jared said, grinning at him. "My sweet Southern mama didn't raise an idiot. Let it not be said that Jared Loring incited Tucker Boone's temper." His smiled faded. "You're really in love with this Alison?"

Tucker straightened and frowned. "Yeah, I really am."

"Well, I mean, hell, aren't you supposed to be smiling? If it was me, I'd be considering the most painless method of suicide, but—what's the problem? Doesn't she love you?"

"I'm sure she does, but she hasn't admitted it to herself yet. Plus, she's got an important career that has always come first with her. Hell, it's a mess, but I have no intention of losing her."

"Then she doesn't stand a chance. Well, I'm happy for you, buddy, because she's obviously what you want. Just make sure this love stuff isn't contagious."

"Mmm," Tucker said, staring off into space.

"Oh, man. Tucker, before you go back into your love-induced trance, can we discuss business here?"

"Huh?" Tucker said, looking at him again.

"Business? The casino?"

"Oh, yeah, sure," he said, nodding. He sat down in a butter-soft leather chair. "It's in the works, Jared. I've had buyers for my offshore oil wells after me to sell for a long time. I got a call late last night from my attorney, and the offer he got is right on the mark. The paperwork is being rushed along. The attorneys are getting everyone to sign on the dotted lines. You and I will buy out the other owners of this place. We split the profits, plus you get a salary for running this show. Miracles Casino will be ours."

"All *right*," Jared said, punching a fist in the air. "We did it."

"You did it. You've been putting this deal together for months. I like it, Jared, I really do. You know that if you really need me here, I'll come, but I figure you can handle just about anything that happens. You're already doing that. Yep, this is good."

Jared leaned forward in his chair. "Do you want kids too? I mean, are you going for the whole nine yards with this Alison?"

"Damn right."

Jared slouched back in his chair. "Amazing. Really amazing. Does she have a last name, or are you so out of it, you forgot to ask?"

Tucker laced his fingers behind his head and smiled up at the ceiling. "Alison Murdock. Beautiful Alison. My Alison. Lord, I do love that little whisper of a woman. She's a tiny package of pure dynamite."

"Well, good luck," Jared said. He shivered. "Just as long as love isn't catching. The very thought of it gives me cold chills. I don't want, need, nor will I allow, some woman to push my buttons."

"Mmm," Tucker said, still smiling at the ceiling.

"Ah, hell, he's gone again," Jared said, shaking his head. "Love is definitely a depleting condition, and I'll pass, thank you very much."

Tucker chuckled. "I hear you mumbling, Jared. Your day will come, pal."

"Not a chance, Tuck."

Tucker dropped his hands and straightened in his chair. "I've got a thousand bucks that says you're wrong. When the right woman crosses your path, you won't be worth a snowball in hell."

"I'm immune to this disease called love, Boone," Jared said.

"A thousand?"

"You're on."

"No time limit. It's an open bet."

"Fine with me." Jared paused. "No, now wait a minute, that's no good. You won't have to pay up until it's time to put the crisp, green bills on my coffin."

"You've got a point." Tucker narrowed his eyes. "One year. I say you'll fall in love within one year from today."

"Easy money. You've got a deal, fool that you are." Jared extended his hand and Tucker shook it. "Now let's break out some champagne and celebrate the fact that you and I are about to be the sole owners of Miracles."

"Bring out the best stuff in the house, Jared. This is a momentous day."

• • •

"Mercer," Alison said, "this is a momentous day. Trust me, you look wonderful, and you'll be so much more comfortable in cooler clothes."

Alison wrung her hands and looked up hopefully at Mercer, who was frowning deeply as he stared into the large mirror in the men's department of the store. She followed his gaze and saw herself reflected standing next to the tall, thin man.

Abraham Lincoln in jeans and a western shirt, she thought, matching Mercer's frown. Somehow it just didn't work. Mercer, bless his heart, looked absolutely ridiculous.

"Oh, my," Alison said, sighing.

"My sentiments exactly, madam," Mercer said, his body as rigid as a board. "This attire is hardly appropriate for a gentleman's gentleman. I do believe, mum, that these jeans, as you call them, could stand up whether I was wearing them or not."

"New jeans are always stiff, Mercer," she said. "You have to wash them a few times to soften them, and . . . oh, never mind. I guess it just isn't . . . you."

"No, mum."

"The shirt is spiffy. Do you like the shirt?" she said, smiling brightly.

"No, mum."

"Oh," she said, frowning again. "So much for that. Do you have any suggestions?"

"Really, Miss Alison, the heat isn't bothering me in the least. I do appreciate your concern, but I'm not having difficulties adjusting to a climate that is so different from England. I do believe I should wear what I'm accustomed to, just be myself."

"Be yourself," Alison said. "Yes, of course. You're

right. Okay, Mercer, go change back into your own things."

"Thank you, mum," he said. He started away. "I say, these jeans even make noise when one walks. A gentleman's gentleman is seen, but definitely not heard, by the rattle of his trousers."

"Good point," Alison said, smiling.

She sat down in a chair. Be yourself, she thought. Mercer Martin was a wise man. But to be yourself, a person had to know exactly who and what he or she was. So, okay, she'd take inventory of Miss Alison Murdock.

Alison straightened in the chair. She was, she thought, a woman who was in love for the first time in her life. She smiled dreamily and pictured magnificent Tucker in her mind's eye, seeing every beautiful, rugged inch of him. His smile was dazzling, his eyes as blue as a Texas summer sky, his body bronzed and proportioned to perfection with taut muscles. When he took her into his arms, when his luscious lips claimed hers, she dissolved into a heap of heated desire. She loved Tucker, wanted to make love with him, be one with him. "Yes, okay," she said, feeling the warm flush on her cheeks, "that covers that part of yourself."

"Are you speaking to me?" a salesman asked.

"What? Oh, no, I'm not. I'm just sitting here waiting for someone."

"Whatever," the young man said, then walked away.

Next on the agenda, Alison continued, tapping a fingertip against her chin, was Alison Murdock, career woman. She really didn't know Alison the career woman, where she was headed, what new road she should take.

"Oh, darn," she said, looking up. Mercer, dressed once more in his dark, three-piece suit, was heading toward her. She got to her feet and forced a smile to her lips. "All set? Let's go for some ice cream, shall we?"

"Yes, mum," he said. "I daresay, I feel more like myself in my proper attire."

"I wish it could be that easy for me."

"Beg your pardon, madam?"

"Nothing, Mercer. Nothing at all. What kind of ice cream do you like?"

Just after midnight Tucker pulled into the driveway, looked at the dark house, and smiled.

Home, he thought. He was home and, oh, damn, it felt good. But even more, Alison was asleep in the house. Alison was there, just as she was meant to be.

He got out of the car, grabbed his suitcase, and started across the lawn. Jared had razzed him unmercifully, Tucker recalled with a chuckle, when he'd said that enough was enough, he was going home to Alison. Jared had finally thrown up his hands in defeat when Tucker had simply smiled and nodded, wholeheartedly agreeing that he was, indeed, a man whose thoughts and actions were being governed by the woman he loved. Love would happen to Jared Loring someday, and then he would understand why Tucker Boone was creeping into his own house in the dead of night.

Tucker unlocked the front door and stepped into the living room. He set his suitcase down and made his way cautiously forward.

"Master Boone?"

"Oh, Lord," Tucker said, jerking in surprise. "Mercer?"

"Yes, sir."

"You scared the— I thought I was being quiet."

"I'm a very light sleeper, sir," Mercer said, turning on the lamp on an end table. He was dressed in pajamas, slippers, and a dark blue robe. "I didn't expect you until late tomorrow, sir."

"I know, but I was going crazy. I had to come back. How's Alison?"

"Fine, sir. She's upstairs asleep. Whatever it was she was involved in for her law firm was concluded. We spent the day in town. Miss Alison agreed that I should continue to wear my own attire, sir. We shopped for jeans, you see, but . . ."

"Okay, as long you're sure you're comfortable the way you usually dress. Did, Alison . . . you know, say anything important?"

"We chatted about many things, sir."

"I'm sure you did, but . . . never mind."

"I understand what you're asking, sir. Miss Alison plans to make only one commitment to one man in her life. She's very firm on that, and it was lovely to hear, sir. She told me that right after we inspected the beasts."

"Beasts?"

"The hideous creatures that were delivered. Cattle."

"I forgot to tell you they were coming."

"I'm very aware of that, sir."

"Sorry," Tucker said, feeling as though he'd been called to the principal's office. "Well, let's forget the cattle for now. Alison actually said that, about committing herself to only one man in her lifetime?"

"Yes, sir. She seemed preoccupied at times, very deep in thought."

"Good, good," Tucker said, nodding. "I just hope she came to the right conclusions. Well, go back to bed, Mercer. I'm sorry I woke you." He started toward the stairs.

"Miss Alison is using the first guest room, sir."

Tucker stopped dead in his tracks and turned to look at Mercer, whose expression was unreadable.

"One wouldn't want to inadvertently walk in on one's guest," Mercer said pleasantly.

"No," Tucker said slowly, "one wouldn't want to inadvertently do that." He chuckled softly. "There are times, Mercer Martin, when you remind me very much of my crafty old grandfather."

"Why thank you, sir. That's truly a compliment." Mercer moved across the room and turned off the lamp. "Good night, Master Boone."

"Good night, Mercer." He paused. "Thank you for everything."

"My pleasure, sir."

Tucker made his way up the stairs in the dark, his eyes becoming accustomed to the lack of light. He stopped outside of the closed door to the first guest room, feeling the increased tempo of his heart.

He shouldn't go in there, he told himself, even though he obviously had Mercer's blessing to do just that. No, he wouldn't do it. But, he did want to look at Alison for a moment while she slept. He'd missed her beyond belief and wanted to see her where she belonged—under his roof.

Tucker turned the knob on the door and slipped inside the room, closing the door with a quiet click behind him. The drapes were opened on the two sets of windows, and the entire expanse was aglow from the silvery luminescence of the moon and stars in the summer sky. And there, asleep in the double bed, was Alison.

Tucker inched forward, blood pounding in his veins, heat gathering low and heavy in his body. He stopped at the edge of the bed and stared down at Alison, a sudden tightness gripping his throat. She lay on her back, the sheet to her waist, her hands fanned next to her head on the pillow. Her nightgown was of a wispy material with tiny straps, and as the moonlight poured over her, he could see her breasts clearly defined beneath the sheer fabric.

Beautiful, Tucker thought. So damn beautiful. Oh, Lord, how he wanted her, ached for her, needed to mesh his body with hers. This was Alison, and he loved her more than he ever would be able to express in words.

Alison watched Tucker from beneath her lashes as she feigned sleep. Her heart was beating so wildly, she was amazed that he couldn't hear it in the quiet room. Tucker was home. She had been dreaming about him; a wonderful, sensuous dream, where he'd taken her into his arms, held her, kissed her, until she was trembling with passion. The opening of the door had awakened her, and she had foggily thought she was imagining the image of Tucker coming into the room.

But, oh, he was real; she knew that now. He was towering above her; so tall, massive, magnificent. She could feel the heat of his gaze and felt her breasts grow heavy, aching for his touch. Low and deep within her, tension coiled, thrummed, with a pulsing cadence. Tucker was home. She loved him. She wanted him.

There was a magical aura to the night, Alison mused wistfully, an ethereal quality, as though she and Tucker had been transported up and away on the silvery beams sent just for them by the moon and stars. In the special place where they could go together, there would be only the two of them—the world, its people, its problems, left far behind. She would be Tucker's, Tucker would be hers, they would be one, and nothing else, no one else, would matter. In that enchanting realm she could take from the guarded chamber of her heart the words she yearned to say to Tucker, give them to him like a gift, in return for the ones he'd spoken to her in kind.

Alison slowly lifted her lashes, then her hands seemed to float upward of their own volition through the silvery mist, reaching for Tucker, welcoming him into her embrace.

"I love you, Tucker Boone," she whispered, hearing the hushed words as though they came from far, far away.

"Ah, Alison," Tucker said with a groan that seemed to come from the very depths of his soul.

Alison loved him! He was filled with joy and sat down on the bed, sliding his hands to her back to raise her to him, her fingers sinking into his thick hair. He held her tightly, her breasts crushed to his chest, filling his senses with the feel of her softness, her sweet, feminine aroma.

"I love you, too, Alison," he said, his voice husky with emotion. "Thank you for loving me, and for saying it. The future is ours now." He moved his head and claimed her mouth in a searing kiss, his tongue slipping between her lips.

Alison's eyes widened in shock as the realization of what she had said jarred her from her dreamy state. She hadn't meant to declare her love for Tucker, not now, not yet. It was too soon. It wasn't fair to Tucker, because she was still confused and frightened about her career, where that part of herself belonged.

Tucker's hands moved from her back to gently cup her breasts, his thumbs stroking the nipples to taut buttons beneath the filmy material of her nightgown. The rhythm of his thumbs was matched by the tantalizing stroking of his tongue with hers, and deep within her another heated pulsing kept tempo, causing her to tremble with the want of him.

No! Wait! she thought frantically. She had to explain, had to tell Tucker that she was lost in a sea of confusion and doubt about her career, that . . .

Tucker pulled the tiny straps of her nightgown from her shoulders, and she lowered her arms to allow him to brush the gown away, freeing her breasts to the silvery night and Tucker's smoldering gaze. He dipped his head and drew one nipple deep into his mouth; tasting, sucking, savoring.

Alison gripped his shoulders and her eyes drifted closed. She arched her back to give him more, to take more. Sensations of ecstasy rocketed through her in waves.

But, no . . . wait . . . she had to tell him . . . he didn't know that she . . . oh, Tucker, yes!

The inner voice of the woman in love spoke louder than the one of the woman of confusion. It stilled the echoes of doubt, pushed them into dark oblivion far from the silvery rapture that belonged to her and Tucker. There were no more tormenting thoughts, there weren't two Alisons, only one, the Alison who loved this man beyond description. There was only the want of him, the need, the heated, aching desire.

There was only the night. And Tucker. And now.

Tucker raised his lips from her breast and took her mouth again, laying her down in the process. Through half-closed eyes Alison watched him as he lifted his head, shifted slightly, then drew her nightgown down and away with the sheet. She was naked before him in a waterfall of silvery radiance.

"You . . ." he began, his voice raspy, "are the most beautiful woman I've ever seen." He skimmed his hands along the gentle slope of her hips, then down the satiny skin of her legs. "Like velvet. So lovely. Mine. I want you so much."

"Yes," she whispered. "Oh, yes, Tucker, I want you too."

He stood and, with visibly shaking hands, shed his clothes. *Easy, Boone,* he told himself. He had to go slow, mustn't rush her. He had to regain his control, make this perfect for Alison, his Alison. Dear Lord, she loved him. This night was the turning point of his life, of their lives, together. They were in love, and they would make love. He'd waited a lifetime, a thousand lifetimes, for this moment. *Easy, Boone.*

Alison's gaze traveled over Tucker's magnificent body, bathed in silvery light. Her breath quickened; he was so strong, so fully aroused, his manhood announcing boldly his want of her, all he would bring to her as a man.

"Oh, Tucker," she said, her voice holding a quality of awe, "you're the one who is beautiful." She lifted her hand toward him. "Come to me, Tucker Boone."

He stretched out next to her, resting his weight on one forearm as his other hand moved slowly, gently, sensuously, over her. His mouth sought first one breast, then the other, drawing each nipple into his mouth in turn. His hand went lower, seeking, finding, sending shock waves of desire through Alison as she moaned in pure pleasure.

Her hands, too, touched, stroked, caressed, and tantalized as she explored and committed to memory all that was Tucker. Their breathing was rough, their hearts pounded, their bodies glistened. But still they held back; anticipating what would come, heightening their passion with the mere thought of what they were about to share.

The curling tension deep within Alison increased to the point of sweet pain. She arched against Tucker's hand, which covered her raging heat, wanting more, needing more. Now.

"Tucker, please."

"I have to be sure you're ready for me, Alison. It's so important that this is good for you. That—"

"Tucker!"

He moved over her, his weight on his arms. Their

eyes met; smoky hues of dark and blue, sending and receiving messages of love and want. Ever so slowly he entered her, watching her face, being certain he was causing her no pain. He waited until her body adjusted to the size and strength of him, gritting his teeth for control, his muscles trembling from forced restraint.

"Oh-h-h, yes," she said, then smiled at him with womanly gentleness.

Alison lifted her hips, and Tucker was lost, his control gone as he began to move within her; deep, so deep, sheathed in her velvety heat. She matched his pace, gloried in their union, which was like none she had ever known. Perfect. So perfect, wondrous—and theirs. Pressure built within her, low, hot, twisting, pulling, taking him farther yet into her willing body. She was tightening around him, surging to the place she knew she must reach.

"Tucker!"

She called his name again, then yet again, as spasms of incredible sensation flung her over the edge of reality. He drove heavily into her once more, then shuddered in his release as he joined her, her name a harsh sound rushing from his lips.

"Alison!"

He collapsed against her, spent, sated, not having the strength to move, his breathing rough. Moments passed as hearts quieted. With his last ounce of energy Tucker moved off her and pulled her close to his side, one hand splayed on her moist back.

"I love you," he said, then further words failed him.

"Yes," was all Alison managed to say.

Seconds ticked into minutes. Neither spoke. They lay serenely in the silvery glow of the night, close, hearts now beating nearly as one.

"Alison," Tucker finally said quietly, "there's so much I want to say to you, should say, but I can't put the words together right now. This night, you, what we shared, meant more to me than I can begin to tell you. Tomorrow we'll talk, make plans, okay? For now we know we love each other—we've told each other that. Everything else will fall into place just as it should be."

"Tucker, I . . . yes, tomorrow we'll talk. Tonight is ours, yours and mine. Nothing else matters right now."

"Go to sleep, my love," he said, kissing her on the forehead. "Oh, and don't worry about Mercer walking in on us in the morning with a breakfast tray. I'm very sure he won't come up here. Mercer learned a thing or two from Jeremy Daniel Boone."

" 'Kay," Alison said sleepily.

"Alison?"

"Yes?"

"One more thing. I wasn't in South America, I went to Vegas. There was no emergency, I was just getting out of your way so you could think without me hovering around. Oh, and Mercer is going to stay on here. That has definitely been settled."

"I see," Alison said softly.

"I just wanted you to know the truth about everything because . . . well, that's how it should be when two people love each other. I'm no expert on the subject, but it seems to me that it's the way it should be. Go to sleep. I promise I won't say another word except that I love you very much. Good night."

"Good night, Tucker," she said. Truth, her mind repeated. Oh, dear Lord, what had she done? Her declaration of love had been real and true, but half of her, the career half, was all confusion. Tucker was keeping nothing from her, and she was hiding so very much from him. She'd tell him, somehow find the courage and strength to tell him that she'd failed.

Within minutes Tucker was asleep, and Alison rested her hand on his chest to feel the steady beat of his heart. She lay staring into the darkness, suddenly aware that clouds must have moved across the sky, for the magical, silvery glow of the moon and stars was gone.

Eight

Sunlight filled the bedroom the next morning when Alison stirred, then opened her eyes. In the next instant she was wide-awake, as memories of the previous night came rushing over her. She turned her head quickly on the pillow to find that Tucker was no longer in the bed with her.

Tucker, she thought, closing her eyes again. Oh, how she loved him, and how glorious their lovemaking had been. Admittedly, her experience with men was limited, but never in her most romantic fantasies had she ever believed that the coming together of a man and woman could be so beautiful. With Tucker she had felt complete, whole, as though part of her had been missing and then found.

And this, she thought, opening her eyes again, was the morning after, the hour of reckoning, the time for regrets and recriminations.

"Well?" Alison said aloud. She knew what was going through her mind, and it sounded ridiculous enough bouncing around her brain without saying it in words to an empty room. The truth of the matter was, she would never regret making love with the man she loved, but she did regret telling the man she loved that she loved him. "See?" she said, wrinkling her nose. "You're a cuckoo, Alison Murdock."

With a sigh she left the bed and headed for the shower, a deep frown on her face.

A little over a half an hour later Alison entered the kitchen dressed in a blue pin-striped suit and a pale blue blouse. Tucker was sitting at the table reading the newspaper, a mug of coffee in his hand. He looked up as she came into the room, then his gaze skimmed over her attire before meeting her eyes again.

"Good morning," he said quietly.

"Hello," she said, managing a small smile.

Tucker got to his feet and came to her, framing her face in his large hands. "I hated to leave you this morning. You looked so beautiful sleeping there next to me. I wanted to wake you, make love to you the entire day, but I had to meet with the work crews."

"Tucker, Mercer—"

"Is off dusting, or whatever he does, in another part of the house. Alison, please, I need to hear you say that you're not sorry about what happened last night."

"Oh, no, Tucker, I'm not sorry. It was wonderful. It was . . . well, you know how it was. I've never felt . . . what I mean is . . ."

"Ditto," he said, smiling, then he lowered his head

and claimed her mouth with his. Oh, thank God, he thought. It was all right; everything was fine. Except . . . He lifted his head. "Why are you dressed like Perry Mason?"

Alison blinked, bringing herself back from the rosy, hazy place she'd been drifting away to. She took a step sideways, forcing Tucker to drop his hands from her face, then went to the stove to pour herself a mug of coffee.

"Well, you said that you've decided to let Mercer stay on here," she said. She walked to the table and sat down. Tucker took his seat across from her. "Therefore I've finished my assignment for Brinker, Brinker, and Abbot." She studied the steaming liquid in her mug. "I would be neglecting my professional duties if I stayed here today. I have to report in to Mr. Brinker." For what? she asked herself glumly. Another tulip-bulb case? "I'm sure you can understand that. I'm so pleased that you've decided to let Mercer stay on. He's such a dear, and he's making every effort to fit in, and he—"

"Whoa," Tucker said, slicing his hand through the air. "Time out. You're talking a hundred miles an hour. Alison, what's wrong?"

She looked up at him quickly. "Nothing. What could be wrong?"

"I don't know. *You* tell *me*." He caught one of her hands with his and trapped it on top of the table. "Alison, let me make something very clear to you just in case there's any doubt in your mind. I love you. I have never loved a woman before, never said those words to anyone but my family and Ricky. I'm not playing games here, not for a second."

"I didn't think you were, Tucker."

"Then it should come as no surprise to you that I'm asking you to marry me, to be my wife, my other half, for the rest of our lives."

"Oh-h-h," Alison said, her bottom lip beginning to tremble.

"Damn, don't cry," he said, squeezing her hand. "Just listen a minute, okay? I know how important your career is to you, and I have no intention of interfering with that. You told me that you love me, which means you must realize there's room in your life for your goals *and* us. It'll work, Alison, because we'll make sure that it does. Mercer will be here to do all the housework, the cooking and stuff, and . . . oh, cripe, now the tears are spilling onto your cheeks. Dammit, talk to me."

Alison pulled her hand free and dashed the tears from her cheeks. "I'm sorry," she said. "I'm being very emotional and dumb. Tucker, couldn't we slow down a little bit?"

He leaned back and crossed his arms over his chest. "Why?"

"Why? Because."

"What kind of an answer is that?" he said, his voice rising.

"The only one I have at the moment," she said miserably.

"There's something missing here," Tucker said, shaking his head. "Something I don't know."

Tucker Boone had just proposed to her. She should be singing from the rooftops with joy instead of crying. Tell him, Alison railed at herself. This was the time.

"Tucker," she said, taking a deep breath, "it's just that things have happened so quickly. I've led a very set, rather quiet life, and all of a sudden everything has changed. You're used to a whirlwind sort of existence, but I need a little time to catch my breath and get used to what has taken place. You can understand that, can't you?"

He smiled. "Can't you get used to all the changes *after* we're married? No, I'm kidding. I do understand. I don't want to, but I do. I recognized Mercer's need to have time to adjust, and I suppose it's something like that. Right?"

"Right," Alison said, smiling brightly. "I'm adjusting. Yes, that's it exactly. My goodness, I haven't even had time to tell my parents about you. Of course, they're away on a cruise they've been saving for for years, but . . . the point is, I simply don't move through life as quickly as you do, despite what Nick says about my not having enough patience. So if you'll just give me a little time . . . ?"

"To adjust," Tucker repeated, frowning slightly.

"Yes."

"How long?"

"Oh, dear," she said, sighing. "I don't know." How long did it take to heal from the hurt of failure? How long did it take to decide on a whole new career goal? "Not long, I hope."

"Nick says *you* don't have patience," Tucker said. "He should get to know *me*. Okay, Alison, I'll try to muster up my patience here."

"Thank you, Tucker, I . . ." She stiffened in her chair. "Nick."

"What about him?"

"He's in trouble. Well, *he's* not in trouble, exactly. Tucker, is there a story in the paper again today about Vincent Munetti?"

"Yep, it's headline news, splashed all over the front page. It says that Brinker, Brinker, and Abbot is representing Munetti, specifically Mr. Brinker, Sr. You said you were helping with the case. Seems to me they could have put your name in the paper."

"I didn't . . . I'm not helping that much," Alison said, then took a sip of coffee. "Just a tad. Nothing worth talking about."

"You're probably being modest," Tucker said. "These hotshot big boys always have genius assistants who pull things out of the fire for them."

"Not this time," Alison muttered. "Tucker, I have to talk to you about Nick."

"Go ahead," he said, then drained his mug.

"Well, you see, Vincent Munetti is Nick's uncle and . . ."

Alison poured out the story of Nick's family and the ramifications Nick had felt all of his life. She left out the part about the missing witness in the Munetti case having been paid off, deciding Nick had not intended that information to go further. Tucker listened intently, nodding several times.

"So you see," she concluded, "Nick has been guilty by association for as long as he can remember. He can't take it anymore, just wants a chance to live in peace. He's going to have to make his mother understand that. Tucker, Nick is big and strong, very intelligent, and is willing to work hard. I was hoping, maybe, well, I thought perhaps you might give him a job somewhere away from Houston where he can have a fresh start, be judged on his own merit."

Tucker looked at her for a long moment. "You really care about this guy, don't you?"

"Yes," she said, nodding. "Oh, please don't misunderstand. Nick is my friend, just my friend."

"I realize that. He's very fortunate to have you for a friend. When you care, you give your all. You've done that for Mercer too. You opened your heart and took him right in. You know, Alison, you don't fit the image I have in my mind of big-time attorneys."

"What?" she said, feeling the color drain from her face.

He shrugged. "I deal with attorneys all the time. Right now, in fact, I'm up to my ears in them because I'm selling my offshore oil wells so I can be a full partner in the Las Vegas casino. Those guys, the attorneys, are sort of clinical. They want facts, no emotional outbursts, no whys and wherefores, just facts. They're busy, always pressed for time. But you? You operate and care on a different level. A people level."

"So I've been told," Alison said miserably.

"If you were representing Munetti, you'd probably decide he was a product of a bad experience in nursery school or something, and none of this is his fault. Oh, forget it. You're obviously a great attorney. I've just never met one who gets so involved in people's lives, who cares so much. It's very refreshing."

It had cost her her dream, Alison thought dismally. It was a liability in her chosen field, not an asset, and there wasn't a darn thing she could do about it.

"Tucker, what about Nick?"

"Well, I'll talk to him, okay? I can't make any

promises until I've spoken with him, sized him up myself. Why don't you give him a call and see if he wants to meet me for lunch? Noon. At the Chimney Stack. They have great hamburgers. I'm going into hamburger withdrawal. I wonder if there's a class Mercer can take on how to cook hamburgers."

"I'll teach him," Alison said, jumping to her feet. She came to the other side of the table and flung her arms around Tucker's neck. "Oh, thank you, thank you, Tucker. You'll like Nick, I just know you will. I have his phone number up in my room. I'll go call him right now." She gave him a fast kiss on the lips.

Tucker lifted his arms to pull her into his embrace and ended up with nothing but empty air as Alison turned and ran from the room.

"Well, hell," he said. She really did care about people so damn much, he mused. That was great, fine, wonderful, when he thought about that depth of caring being directed at him, their children. But in a court of law? They'd gobble her up. She needed a tough outer crust that just wasn't there. Yet Brinker was bringing her along, showing her the ropes. Was the guy blind? Couldn't he see that Alison wasn't cut out for no-holds-barred battles?

Tucker shook his head, then got to his feet and went to refill his coffee mug. He leaned against the counter and sipped the hot liquid.

Alison wanted more time to think, he thought. Damn. He wanted to marry her right now, today, yesterday. Well, he had no choice but to wait. For a while. There was definitely a limit to his patience. They loved each other, made fantastic, beautiful love together, so what was the holdup here? It was time to get on with their lives together. But he'd wait. For now.

Alison came dashing back into the room, bringing Tucker back from his reverie.

"It's all set," she said. "Nick will meet you for lunch."

Tucker nodded, then set his mug on the counter.

"I've got to go," Alison said. "I really must report to work."

"First you need to report in to me," Tucker said. "Come here, my Alison."

And she went. As Tucker opened his arms to her she moved into his embrace as naturally as breathing. She met his lips, his tongue, pressed her body tightly to his, and returned his hungry kiss in total abandon. Thoughts fled, passions soared, and there was only the two of them in the private world they created.

"Oh-h-h, Lord," Tucker said when he finally lifted his head, "this is going to be a very long day. What time will you be home?"

"Home?" Alison said, very aware that her knees were trembling, her cheeks flushed with desire.

"Here. Home."

"Oh, but I . . . that is, I'm going back to my apartment tonight."

"Why?"

"Well, goodness, Tucker, I can't just move in here."

"Alison, for crying out loud, we love each other, and I want you to marry me. We made love last night, remember?"

"Shh. Shh," she said, flapping her hands at him. "Mercer might hear you."

"Mercer knows what's going on. I want you here with me, dammit. You belong here—in this house, and in my bed at night."

"You said you'd give me some time!"

Tucker stared up at the ceiling for a long moment in an attempt to rein in his rising temper. He looked at her again. "O-kay," he said slowly, "we'll do this your way for now. I'll pick you up at your apartment at seven, and we'll go out to dinner. Someplace fancy."

"Thank you, Tucker," she said, smiling. "I must go now. And thank you for agreeing to talk to Nick."

"No problem. I love you, Alison."

"Yes," she said, backing up. "Yes, I know you do. I'll . . . I'll see you tonight. 'Bye." She turned and hurried from the room.

A deep frown settled onto Tucker's face as he stood alone in the quiet kitchen. Alison hadn't said it, he realized. Not once that morning had she said that she loved him. She'd whispered those precious words to him one time the previous night but hadn't declared her love for him since. Something . . . something just wasn't right here. He had a knot in his gut that told him that things were not as they should be.

"Dammit," he said.

"Sir?" Mercer said, coming into the kitchen.

"Oh, hi, Mercer," Tucker said.

"I saw Miss Alison leave, sir."

"Yeah, she went to work. I won't be here for lunch today. I have to meet a guy in town."

"Very good, sir."

"I wish *I* was convinced that things are very good," Tucker said, running his hand over the back of his neck. "I just have this feeling that something isn't as it should be." He shook his head. "Well, all I can do is stay alert, pay attention. I'm going to go work on the corrals, Mercer." He started toward the door, then stopped. "Oh, I won't be home for dinner, either. I'm taking Alison out."

"Yes, sir. A quiet, romantic restaurant, I trust?"

"The most romantic I can find."

"Excellent, sir. That will be very appropriate after the flowers."

"What flowers?"

"The ones you might consider sending Miss Alison in the middle of the afternoon, sir."

"Oh, *those* flowers," Tucker said, chuckling. "Good idea. I'll tend to that while I'm in town for lunch. Anything else I should do?"

"That should take care of today and this evening very nicely, sir."

"If you say so, Mercer. Lord, being in love is complicated."

"But worth it, sir."

"Definitely," Tucker said, starting toward the door again. He nodded decisively.

Alison sat in her quiet office and studied every inch of the nicely furnished room as though seeing it for the first time. She was not, she realized, the same person she had been the last time she'd sat behind this desk. She was now a woman in love who had made love with the man of her heart. She was also a woman in turmoil about her career.

She was also, she decided, sick and tired of thinking about her imaginary roads. Hers had always been so clear in her mind to the point that she'd seen it paved with shiny yellow bricks; success personified was to have been Alison Murdock, the greatest trial lawyer in the history of trial lawyers.

She picked up a pencil and began to doodle on a pad of paper. She had nothing to do to occupy her time, she thought dismally. She'd left a message for Mr. Brinker with his secretary, saying that Alison was ready to be assigned a new case. The secretary had poked her head in the door an hour later and announced that Mr. Brinker was still in conference regarding the Munetti case, so why didn't Alison get caught up on her paperwork? That was dandy, except that when a person had a paralegal assistant as efficient as Nick, there was no paperwork left to do.

"I miss you, Nick," Alison said. No, she wasn't going to start talking to herself again. That was so unprofessional and so immature. "Yes, grow up, Alison."

Grow up, Alison.

Her own words bounced back at her, beating against her mind. Oh, she thought, stiffening in her chair, her eyes widening in horror. Was it possible that she was . . . was behaving like a child, a spoiled brat who was pouting because things hadn't gone the way she'd decided they ought to go? Was she wallowing in self-pity to the point that any minute now she might stick her thumb in her mouth, throw herself on the floor, and kick her feet?

Grow up, Alison.

"You care on a different level," Tucker had said. "You don't fit the image in my mind of big-time attorneys. You care on a people level."

"Wake up and smell the coffee," Nick had said.

And Mr. Brinker had said, "You care deeply about people, and it shows. You're excellent on a one-to-one basis. Devote yourself to where your talents lie."

Alison pressed her fingertips to her throbbing temples as the multitude of voices tumbled through her mind. She cared about people? But she'd stood in judgment of them! She, big-shot Alison, had shaken her head in dismay at their lack of ambition, the fact that the people around her weren't living up to their potential. People she claimed to care for and love: her parents, Nick, even Tucker when she'd first met him.

Who in the blue blazes did she think she was?

How dare she act so high-and-mighty?

Who was she, who now stood on a road crumbled into dust, to find unworthy the roads that others had chosen? When had she ever had the right to do that?

Grow up, Alison.

Oh, yes, she thought, that was exactly what she had to do. She'd made terrible mistakes with her tunnel vision. She'd ignored the signs and signals warning her that she was on the wrong path and plowed ahead, anyway. And then she'd pitched a childish fit when it hadn't gone exactly her way. She'd never even tried to understand her parents choices, had never considered that there might be circumstances holding Nick back from his dreams. She'd labeled Tucker as a lazy vagabond at their first meeting and changed her mind only when he'd so dramatically shown himself to be different.

A failure?

No, dammit, Alison thought, smacking the desk with her hand. *She was not a failure!* Yes, all right, she had failed to chose the proper goal for herself, but so had a multitude of others first starting out. The failure would come only if she refused to pull back, regroup, head in a direction that was more appropriate for her. She was a people person, and there were people out there who needed her kind of caring. There was a place for her. And this time, *this time*, she'd make certain her goal included taking quiet moments to smell the flowers.

"Flowers," a woman said, coming into the room. Alison jumped in her chair. "You've been keeping things from me, Alison." She placed a long white box tied in a silver ribbon on Alison's desk. "Who is he?"

"Flowers?" Alison said, staring at the box. "I was just thinking about flowers, Trudy."

"So open the box," Trudy said, waving her hands at her. "Oh, I love flowers. I think the last I had was my wedding bouquet. My husband, the rat, gave me a vacuum cleaner for my birthday. Last Christmas he gave me a tool kit in case anything needed repairing while he was out of town. If I didn't love him so much, I'd shoot him. Alison, would you open the box?"

"Oh, yes, of course." She slid the silver ribbon off, lifted the lid, then brushed back the green tissue. "Oh, my."

"White roses!" Trudy said. "Do you know what white roses cost? No, forget that. Don't be practical at a romantic time—it spoils the whole thing." She sighed. "A dozen white roses, and each one has a tiny silver bow tied to it." She leaned forward. "That means something, right? It's significant, a private message between lovers. Are you going to tell me?"

"No."

"Didn't think so. So much for you, Alison Murdock. I'll leave you to your romantic interlude while I go conjure up images of my vacuum cleaner." She spun around and stomped out of the room.

Alison reached for the card that was nestled in the box and drew it from the envelope with trembling fingers.

" 'Silver moonlight and you,' " she read with a whisper. " 'I love you. Tucker.' Oh, heavens," she said, her eyes filling with tears. "How beautiful." She lifted the box and inhaled the enchanting aroma of the roses. "I love you, too, Tucker Boone. Tonight I'm going to tell you everything. Everything. I'm going to be just fine now, Tucker, you'll see. *We're* going to be fine, I promise you that. I . . . oh, Alison, would you please, *please*, quit talking to yourself?"

She put the lid back on the box, picked it up, took her purse from the bottom drawer, and left the office. She stopped at Trudy's desk.

"I'm leaving for the day," Alison said. "All my paperwork is done, and I have nothing to do. I am, therefore, going out to buy a new dress for a very special evening with a magnificent man."

"Now you're speaking my language, cookie," Trudy said. "Go for it, Alison. Lordy, this is great. I was so afraid you were going to turn into just another stuffy old lawyer."

"That isn't about to happen. I," Alison said, sticking her nose in the air, "am a people person."

"Oh, I always knew that," Trudy said. "I just didn't think *you* knew it."

"I do now," Alison said quietly. "I chose the wrong road for myself, Trudy, but I'm going to find the proper one this time, and it's going to be lined with flowers."

Trudy smiled. "Fantastic. Have a wonderful evening, Alison."

"It's going to be glorious," she said with a big smile. "Absolutely glorious."

Tucker slid back into the booth and looked at Nick, who sat across from him.

"I'm sorry that took so long," Tucker said. "I called Jared, and he put me on hold while he made a few calls himself. He was, in short, checking you out."

Nick smiled. "I don't blame him."

"Jared knows people in high places, as well as people, shall we say, in low places. The crazy part is, they're all there for him if he needs them. Big shots, sleazeballs, everything in between, Jared knows them. He led a very active, interesting life before settling in at Miracles five years ago. Jared and I go way back, but there's a hunk of time in there after we graduated from college, when we didn't see much of each other, and he doesn't often talk of those years."

"And you don't press."

"Nope," Tucker said, shaking his head. "He'd just pop up sometimes wherever I was in the world, and we'd have a good time, as though we'd seen each other the week before."

"Friendships like that are rare," Nick said.

"I know. Jared knows that too. Anyway, Nick, you are, according to Jared's sources, exactly who and what you told me you are. You're as clean as the Ivory Snow baby, but your family . . . well, they're a different ball game."

"Tell me about it," Nick said, shaking his head.

"What Jared likes about it," Tucker went on, "is that while the feds and others know you're not involved in your family's doings, the word on the street is that you're still a Capoletti, and to take you on could very well mean squaring off against your whole clan. They're not real sure where you stand with your relatives, but no one would be in a rush to find out. That tickles Jared's sense of humor."

"Oh, yeah?" Nick said, smiling. "I'm glad someone is enjoying this. I've had enough."

"I don't blame you. Okay, bottom line: You've got a job at Miracles if you want it."

"Doing what?"

Tucker shrugged. "Jared will know five minutes after he meets you, has a chance to see you for himself. It won't be gofer work, be assured of that. Jared and I are buying out the other owners of the casino, and some of their people are splitting. We'd be glad to have you with us, Nick."

Nick looked at Tucker for a long moment. "Thank you. I mean that very sincerely. It'll take me a few days to wrap things up here, then I'm on my way to Vegas. You won't be sorry, Tucker."

"I know that."

"I promised Alison I'd say good-bye to her before I left."

"No problem," Tucker said, grinning at him. "I

trust you with my lady, even if you are a hot-blooded Italian. Alison is something, isn't she?"

"The best," Nick said, nodding. "I'm glad she has you, Tucker. She'd be furious if she heard me say this, but Alison needs someone to . . . well, sort of watch over her." Nick rolled his eyes heavenward. "She'd strangle me for saying that. She's vulnerable and too trusting to be moving among some of those barracuda attorneys. Well, at least I can go away knowing you're with her, and knowing that Brinker isn't going to screw up and turn her loose to be torn to shreds in a courtroom with a trial case."

Tucker frowned. "What do you mean? Being a trial lawyer is Alison's goal, her dream."

"Oh, hell," Nick said. "Damn, I was sure she'd told you by now. Look, forget I said anything, okay?"

"Not a chance, Nick," Tucker said, his jaw tightening. "What in the hell is going on here?"

"Give me a break, Tucker. I'm a Capoletti, remember? I know how to keep my mouth shut. I just assumed you knew, that's all. What are you going to tell Jared? Old Nick can be trusted until a little muscle leans on him? No way."

"I understand where you're coming from, Nick, but you have to see my side of this. I'm in love with Alison, want to marry her and spend the rest of my life with her. Something is wrong. I've felt it, sensed it, but I can't help her if I don't know what it is."

"Marry her?"

"Marry her," Tucker said firmly.

Nick stared out the window, a deep frown on his face that showed he was warring with his own thoughts. "I think," he said finally, switching his gaze back to Tucker, "that she needs help with this, needs you to tell her she's not a failure. That's what's cutting her up inside, the thought of having to tell you that she is—in her eyes, anyway—a failure. Okay, Tucker, here it is."

"And I'm listening," Tucker said, leaning slightly forward.

"Look," Nick said, "I can't stand to see Alison so unhappy. She isn't going to be a trial lawyer, not ever. Brinker told her flat out. I've known it for months. Alison just doesn't have that killer instinct needed for the rapid-fire cross-examination of witnesses. She is sensational with people on a one-to-one basis. But a courtroom? A jury? No. That was her dream, and it isn't going to happen. She feels she failed. She feels she's fallen short of what she claimed to be when she met you. She's always had an adversion for settling for less, and that's exactly what she's going to have to do. She's not going to be a trial lawyer."

"How long . . . how long has she known the truth?" Tucker said, a painful knot tightening in his stomach.

"Just a couple of days."

No! Oh, Lord, no! Tucker thought, but all he said was, "I see." He forced a smile. "I appreciate your telling me, Nick. It explains . . . a great deal."

"I hope I did the right thing."

"You did. Believe me, Nick, you did."

Nine

The dress was the most beautiful creation she'd ever owned, Alison thought as she stood in her bedroom staring at her reflection in the mirror. She wasn't totally convinced that the image bouncing back was really hers.

She was silvery moonlight.

The full-length gown left one shoulder entirely bare as it draped softly above her breasts to glide over her other shoulder. The bloused bodice was a glittering array of silver sequins that caught the light and twinkled like stars in a summer-night sky. The waist was snug, and the silver chiffon gently hugged her hips before flaring slightly to fall to the tops of silver heels.

Alison blinked, blinked again, and when the person in the mirror did the same, she actually believed that she had been transformed into the sophisticated woman before her.

"All grown-up," she whispered. It would take more than a heavenly dress, she knew, to carry out the changes needed within her. The gown was an outward sign of maturity; the inner growth would come with time and, yes, patience. But there was no doubt in her mind that her love for Tucker Boone came from the proper place, the part of herself that was woman in full bloom, like the exquisite white roses. Alison, the woman in love, knew herself to be equal to Tucker, the man she had chosen to share her life with.

Alison picked up a silver clutch purse and left the bedroom, turning off the light as she went. It was Alison, the career woman, she had come to realize, who was not fully mature, who had been narrow-minded, immature, and judgmental.

Well, all that was over, she thought decisively. She now clearly saw what she had done wrong, was willing to admit it and to start to change. And tonight she would explain it all to Tucker, keep no more secrets from the man she loved with every breath in her body. In just a few minutes now Tucker would be with her.

Tucker stepped out of the elevator on Alison's floor and walked slowly down the hall toward her door. His muscles ached, he realized. When he'd returned to the mini-ranch after having had lunch with Nick, Tucker had worked for hours on the corrals. He'd pushed his body to the limit, then beyond, trying desperately to quiet the screaming voices of doubt in his mind.

But he knew it hadn't worked. He'd gotten nothing for his efforts but repaired corrals, a beat-up body, and a darker tan. The voices refused to be stilled, the questions regarding Alison and her love for him raged on, and the twisting pain in his gut grew more intense.

He felt as though he were teetering on the edge of a dark abyss into which he might fall at any given moment. The wrong answers from Alison would hurl him over into black oblivion and loneliness. But he *would* have the answers, the truth—he had to, for the doubts, the unknowns, were eating him alive.

Tucker stopped outside of Alison's door and drew a hand down his face as he took a shuddering breath. *Oh, Alison, please,* he thought with a rush of panic, *don't let all of this, all we've shared, prove to be a lie.*

He knocked on the door.

Alison spun around at the sound of the knock, a smile on her face. Tucker was there. A part of her was nervous, and a flock of butterflies flitted through her stomach. She was to bare her soul to this man, admit to the flaws of her own character. Yet she knew she would gain strength and courage from remembering how Tucker had revealed his pain and fears when he'd told her about Ricky. His revelations had been a precious gift of trust, and tonight she would return that gift in kind.

She crossed the room and opened the door.

Tucker.

Magnificent Tucker.

In a perfectly tailored gray suit, burgundy silk shirt, and a gray and burgundy striped tie he was, Alison decided, the most beautiful man she'd ever seen. His skin was bronzed deeper by the sun, his sun-streaked hair a tad too long by yuppie standards. The suit accentuated his rugged, muscular build; muscles gained by hard labor, not by hours spent in a health club. He was Tucker. And she loved him.

"Hello, Tucker," she said softly, then stepped back. "Come in. You look wonderful."

Tucker came into the room, his gaze sweeping over her as she shut the door and turned to face him. Heated desire gathered in his body, but he willed it away, telling himself he had to keep a clear head, his thoughts centered on finding out the truth. But she was so lovely; a moonbeam, a silvery, twinkling star. She was Alison. And he loved her.

"Thank you for the flowers," Alison said.

"You're welcome," he said quietly. "That dress . . . you're beautiful, Alison. Incredibly beautiful, like moonlight and stars."

"That's why I chose it. It reminded me of our night together in the moonlight, and so did your flowers. Our minds seem to be on the same wavelength."

"Are they?" he said, his jaw tightening slightly.

Something was wrong, Alison thought. She could feel the tension emanating from Tucker, could see the coiled set to his body. There was a strange, haunting look in his blue eyes as he stared at her, as though he were attempting to seek the path to her soul. And he hadn't touched her, hadn't pulled her into his strong arms to kiss and hold her. Dear heaven, what was the matter with him?

"Would you like a drink?" she said, knowing her voice was no longer steady. "Wine? Scotch?"

"Scotch. Neat."

"I'll get it. Why don't you sit down?"

"No, I'll stand."

"Oh, well, fine. I'll be right back." She hurried into the kitchen.

"Make mine a double," Tucker called after her. He unbuttoned his jacket and jammed his hands into his pockets, knowing it would be the only way to keep from hauling Alison into his arms and kissing her until neither of them could breathe. Lord, he was wired, so tense that his teeth ached. His entire future, his happiness, his newly discovered hopes and dreams were there with him on the edge of that dark abyss.

Alison returned to the living room carrying Tucker's drink and a glass of white wine for herself. She managed a small smile as she handed him the hefty serving of liquor, then immediately sat down in a straight-backed chair as her trembling knees threatened to give way.

"So!" she said a trifle too loudly. "How did your meeting with Nick go?"

Fine, up until the last few minutes of it, Tucker thought dryly. "Fine." He took a deep swallow of the liquor. "Nick is going to Las Vegas to work with my partner, Jared Loring, at Miracles, our casino. Nick said he'd say good-bye to you before he left."

"Oh, Tucker, thank you for helping him."

He shrugged. "There's nothing to thank me for. Nick's a good man. He's had a bum rap laid on him for a long time. Jared and I both feel that Nick will be a real asset to Miracles. It will be up to Nick to decide as time passes whether he likes the atmosphere, the borderline insanity that goes along with the casino, the town. He can always bail out if he feels he's made a mistake."

"Yes, he could," Alison said, staring into her glass, "and he'd have the maturity to admit to that mistake if it came to that." She looked up at Tucker. "Not everyone has that kind of maturity, Tucker."

"Is that a fact?" he said, then drained his glass in two deep swallows. He slammed the glass onto the end table with such force that Alison jerked in her chair, nearly spilling her wine. "And the others, the ones who aren't that mature?" he said, a rough edge to his voice. "What do they do? Scramble around for a safe backup, settle for less, deciding it's better than nothing? They've blown it, right? Their master plan got screwed up, so they have to resort to lousy plan B, rather than end up empty-handed. Is that how it works, Alison?"

Alison set her glass on the table with a shaking hand and stared up at Tucker with wide eyes. He met her gaze, blue eyes flashing.

"You know," she said, her voice hushed. "You know, don't you, that I'll never be a trial lawyer. Nick must have told you."

"He assumed I knew!" Tucker roared. "Dumb Nick, huh? Thinking there were no secrets between us? Of course, that's what I thought, too, jerk that I am.

So there I sat hearing that your almighty career was, in your eyes, blown to smithereens, and not knowing a damn thing about it."

"Tucker, I—"

"Funny thing about the timing of it all, Alison," he said, beginning to pace the floor.

"Timing?" she said, her eyes riveted on him. "What do you mean?"

He stopped in front of her and leaned over, gripping the arms of the chair, pinning her in place. A pulse point throbbed in the strong column of his tanned neck, and his eyes appeared to Alison to be as cold as ice. His voice was ominiously low when he spoke, his face only inches from hers.

"*You* tell *me*. Tell me about the timing of your career being shot to hell, and you whispering to me in the moonlight that you loved me. You remember saying that, don't you? It was just before I made love with you. Interesting part is, you haven't told me you loved me since those words got me into bed with you. Hell, I even asked you to marry me. It's too bad you had to settle for less, Alison, had to resort to plan B, life with Tucker Boone, because you made a mistake in your career choice."

"Dear God," Alison said, her voice trembling, "is that what you think? Do you honestly believe that I viewed you, our love, our future together, as settling for less? Do you think I schemed, worked it all out so that I could have you, since I wasn't to achieve my career goals? Tucker? Is that what you believe?"

"I don't know what I believe!" he yelled, levering himself up from the chair to tower over her. "I'm waiting for you to explain it to me, the timing, waiting to hear the truth!"

Never before had she felt so cold, Alison thought hazily, wrapping her hands around her elbows, so empty, so bruised, as though struck by a physical blow. She stared at a button in the middle of Tucker's shirt, willing herself not to cry. She couldn't move, could scarcely breathe, and unshed tears ached in her throat.

This wasn't happening, she told herself frantically. She'd dozed off, was having a nightmare. She'd awaken, go to the door, and Tucker would be there. He'd draw her into the strong, safe haven of his arms and kiss her until their passions were raging flames. No, of course this wasn't happening. It was too harsh, too much to bear. Tucker couldn't be doubting the sincerity of her love, standing in judgment of her words and actions.

Grow up, Alison.

Alison's head snapped up as though another person had entered the room and spoken those now familiar words. Her gaze collided with Tucker's, and for a brief, fleeting moment she saw deep and devastating pain in his blue eyes. In the next instant his eyes were as cold as ice again as he stood above her, waiting for her to speak.

"Nothing to say?" Tucker asked, his voice gritty. "Does your silence mean I've hit the nail right on the head? Sorry to spoil your grand plans, Alison, but I'm bailing out of this fiasco. I won't rank as second choice for anyone, not even you."

Grow up, Alison. This wasn't a nightmare, it was real, and it was wrong! She was a woman, not a child, and this time she had made no mistake; Tucker Boone was the man she loved with all that she was. This time she wasn't going to weep and moan, wring her hands in self-pity as defeat crushed her. She'd deserved the final outcome of her aborted career plans because she'd been too immature to face the truth from the beginning.

But, by damn, not this time!

"Ah, hell, I'm getting out of here," Tucker said, starting toward the door. "It's over, finished. I've been the fool of the century."

As Tucker reached for the doorknob Alison surged to her feet.

"Don't you move another inch, Tucker Boone," she said, her voice low but ringing with authority.

He hesitated, his hand just above the doorknob, then he shifted to face her, his features tight, his eyes narrowed as he looked at her. Tension seemed to crackle between them like electric wires as they stood a room apart, staring at each other.

Alison took a deep breath and lifted her chin. "I could rant and rave at you, Tucker, accuse you of having no trust in me, in my love, tell you that through a lack of trust you've destroyed all we might have had together. But I won't say those things because it would be childish of me. I'd be shifting all the blame to you, then I could feel oh, so very sorry for myself."

She clasped her hands tightly together to hide their trembling. "Your accusations," she went on, "your questions, are based on facts and events that were happening around you. You faced them, sought answers, are determined to know if you made a mistake when you chose to love me. I respect that, and you, for being mature enough, man enough, to realize you could very well have chosen wrong."

Tucker continued to stare at her with narrowed eyes, every muscle in his body coiled and tense.

"I didn't have that kind of maturity, you see," Alison said, her voice quivering slightly, "when it came to my career. I felt as if I were a failure, and I didn't know how to tell you."

Tucker shook his head. "You're not a—"

"Failure?" she said, interrupting. "Oh, I know that now. I made the wrong career choice, pure and simple. There's a place for me in law, and I'll find it, weighing all the options with the maturity I was lacking before."

"Alison—"

"No, let me finish." She took another deep breath, and her voice was firm and steady when she spoke again. "Yes, let me finish, and you had better listen to every word, buster."

Tucker's eyes widened in shock.

"I'm admitting that I viewed my career through childish eyes. But my love for you? That came from a different place within me, a womanly place; mature and real and equal to you, the man I love. You were never second choice, Tucker. I never saw our life, our future, our love, as settling for less. I love you as you deserve to be loved, and separate and apart from the chaos of my career. I love you woman to man, just as it should be. That is the truth."

Her eyes filled with sudden tears. "And," she said, her voice trembling, "in my opinion, Tucker Boone, if you throw our love away now, you will be making the worst mistake of your life. We can have it all—the hopes, the dreams, the future—if you still want it. If you choose the wrong road and go down it without me, then . . . then I'll consider you the biggest, dumbest doofus I've ever known." Tears spilled onto her cheeks. "And that, Mr. Boone, is all I have to say to you." She dashed the tears from her cheeks.

Silence hung in the air like an oppressive weight for several long, suffocating moments.

Then a smile began to creep onto Tucker's lips. "Doofus? The biggest, dumbest doofus?"

Anger flashed in Alison's tear-filled eyes. "Don't you dare laugh at me, Tucker Boone. Just shut up, shut up, shut up! You wanted to leave? Well, there's the door. Go!"

"No."

"What?"

He started slowly toward her. "I'm not leaving. Not ever. You would have been justified in accusing me of not loving you enough to trust you, but you didn't do that." He stopped in front of her. "I realize now that *I* have some growing up to do, things to learn about loving and being loved in return." He cradled her face in his hands and gently stroked the tears from her cheeks with his thumbs. "Forgive me, Alison," he said, his voice husky with emotion, "for doubting you. Forgive me, please, for my mistakes. I love you, I need you with me on that road for the rest of my life."

"Oh, Tucker," Alison said, nearly choking on a sob.

"Will you marry me, Alison Murdock? Will you be

my wife, the mother of my children, my other half?" Tears glistened in his eyes. "Oh, God, Alison, please?"

She flung her arms around his neck. "Yes! Oh, Tucker, yes. I love you so very much."

He dropped his hands to her back and pulled her to him, his mouth coming down hard on hers. She leaned into him, savoring his heat and strength, his taste and aroma. The kiss gentled as the tension ebbed from Tucker's body, and the embrace became sensuous, speaking of hurts forgotten and desire rekindled. His hands roamed over the glittering, silvery sequins of her dress, then lower to her buttocks, to nestle her to the cradle of his hips. His arousal was heavy against her, announcing his want and need of her.

He lifted his head a fraction of an inch. "Dinner."

"Not hungry," she said with a little puff of air.

"*I'm* hungry."

"Oh."

"For you, only for you, Alison."

"Oh."

He trailed nibbling kisses down the side of her slender throat, then across her bare shoulder before returning to speak close to her lips.

"Moonbeams are delicious," he said, his voice gritty with passion. "I want to make love to you now. Right now."

"Oh." She blinked, then smiled. "That sounds lovely."

He swung her up into his arms and held her tightly to his chest. A grin split across his face. "Doofus?"

Alison laughed as she wound her arms around his neck. "We lawyers are extremely articulate, sir. That is a highfalutin word."

"Yes, but can you cook hamburgers?"

"What am I going to do with you?" Alison asked, smiling.

His expression grew serious. "Just love me. Just love me forever."

"Guaranteed," she said softly. "Forever is where our road will take us."

He brushed his lips across hers, then carried her into the bedroom. Their lovemaking was slow, sweet, and beautiful. Lips and hands caressed; words of endearment and commitment were whispered over and over.

Although the Houston sky was cloaked in dark clouds, the bedroom seemed to glow with the silvery luminescence of the moon and a million twinkling stars.

Epilogue

Alison hurried out of the back door and across the grass to where Tucker stood leaning his arms on the top of one of the corrals. A glistening black horse pranced in the enclosure.

"Tucker," Alison called, then rushed to his side. "Oh, he came. What a gorgeous horse."

Tucker slid his arm around her waist, pulled her up against him, and kissed her deeply. Alison was trembling when he released her.

"Delightful kiss, Mr. Boone," she said, smiling up at him, "but you're a sweaty man. You just grunged up my work clothes."

He laughed. "You're whipping those jazzy words on me again, Mrs. Boone. How was your day at Legal Aid?"

"Marvelous. I'm helping people, Tucker, and it feels so good, so right. I must remember to thank Nick for suggesting I look into Legal Aid. Could we call Nick and Jared tonight at Miracles?"

"Sure. I'll tell them about my horse here," he said, switching his gaze back to the animal. "He's the reason I'm so sweaty. We had a debate about whether or not he was going into that corral. He's something, and we are going to be one helluva breeding ranch because of him. That fella will produce top-notch babies, my love."

"He's not the only one," Alison said.

"What?" Tucker said, looking at her quickly.

"I just came from the doctor. We're going to have a baby."

Tucker's eyes widened. "You're kidding. No, you're not kidding." He swung her up into his arms and kissed her. "A baby! This is fantastic. A baby!" He strode toward the house.

Alison laughed. "Tucker, put me down. You're sweaty, remember?"

"We'll shower. Together. Lord, I'm the luckiest man on the face of the earth. I have you, your love, and now . . ." Mercer came out of the back door. "Hey, Mercer, guess what? We're going to have a baby!"

"Very, very good, madam, sir. I say, that is jolly fine news."

And then to the shock and delight of Alison and Tucker, Mercer Martin smiled.

THE EDITOR'S CORNER

Have you been having fun with our **HOMETOWN HUNK CONTEST**? If not, hurry and join in the excitement by entering a gorgeous local man to be a LOVESWEPT cover hero. The deadline for entries is September 15, 1988, and contest rules are in the back of our books. Now, if you need some inspiration, we have six incredible hunks in our LOVESWEPTs this month . . . and you can dream about the six to come next month . . . to get you in the mood to discover one of your own.

First next month, there's Jake Kramer, "danger in the flesh," the fire fighter hero of new author Terry Lawrence's **WHERE THERE'S SMOKE, THERE'S FIRE,** LOVESWEPT #288. When Jennie Cisco sets eyes on Jake, she knows she's in deep trouble—not so much because of the fire he warns her is racing out of control toward her California retreat, as because of the man himself. He is one tough, yet tender, and decidedly sexy man . . . and Jennie isn't the least bit prepared for his steady and potent assault on her senses and her soul. A musician who can no longer perform, Jenny has secluded herself in the mountains. She fiercely resists Jake's advances . . . until she learns that it may be more terrifying to risk losing him than to risk loving him. A romance that blazes with passion!

Our next hunk-of-the-month, pediatrician Patrick Hunter, will make you laugh along with heroine Megan Murphy as he irresistibly attracts her in **THANKSGIVING,** LOVESWEPT #289, by Janet Evanovich. In this absolutely delightful romance set in Williamsburg, Virginia, at turkey time, Megan and Dr. Pat suddenly find themselves thrown together as the temporary parents of an abandoned baby. Wildly attracted to each

(continued)

other, both yearn to turn their "playing house" into the real thing, yet circumstances *and* Megan's past conspire to keep them apart . . . until she learns that only the doctor who kissed her breathless can heal her lonely heart. A love story as full of chuckles as it is replete with the thrills of falling in love.

Move over Crocodile Dundee, because we've got an Aussie hero to knock the socks off any woman! Brig McKay is a hell-raiser, to be sure, and one of the most devastatingly handsome men ever to cross the path of Deputy Sheriff Millie Surprise, in LOVESWEPT #290, **CAUGHT BY SURPRISE,** by Deborah Smith. Brig has to do some time in Millie's jail, and after getting to know the petite and feisty officer, he's determined to make it a life sentence! But in the past Millie proved to be too much for the men in her life to take, and she's sure she'll turn out to be an embarrassment to Brig. You'll delight in the rollicking, exciting, merry chase as Brig sets out to capture his lady for all time. A delight!

You met that good-looking devil Jared Loring this month, and next Joan Elliott Pickart gives you his own beguiling love story in **MAN OF THE NIGHT,** LOVESWEPT #291. Tabor O'Casey needed Jared's help to rescue her brother, who'd vanished on a mysterious mission, and so she'd called on this complicated and enigmatic man who'd befriended her father. Jared discovers he can refuse her nothing. Though falling as hard and fast for Tabor as she is falling for him, Jared suspects her feelings. And, even in the midst of desperate danger, Tabor must pit herself against the shadowed soul of this man and dare to prove him wrong about her love. A breathlessly beautiful romance!

Here is inspirational hunk #5: Stone Hamilton, one glorious green-eyed, broad-shouldered man and the hero of **TIME OUT,** LOVESWEPT #292, by Patt

(continued)

Bucheister. Never have two people been so mismatched as Stone and beautiful Whitney Grant. He's an efficiency expert; she doesn't even own a watch. He's supremely well-organized, call him Mr. Order; she's delightfully scattered, call her Miss Creativity. Each knows that something *has* to give as they are drawn inexorably into a love affair as hot as it is undeniable. Just how these two charming opposites come to resolve their conflicts will make for marvelous reading next month.

Would you believe charismatic, brawny, handsome, *and* rich? Well, that's just what hero Sam Garrett is! You'll relish his all-out efforts to capture the beautiful and winsome Max Strahan, in **WATER WITCH,** LOVESWEPT #293, by Jan Hudson. Hired to find water on a rocky Texas ranch, geologist Max doesn't want anyone to know her methods have nothing to do with science—and everything to do with the mystical talent of using a dowsing stick. Sam's totally pragmatic—except when it comes to loving Max, whose pride and independence are at war with her reckless desire for the man she fears will laugh at her "gift." Then magic, hot and sweet, takes over and sets this glorious romance to simmering! A must-read love story.

Enjoy all the hunks this month and every month!

Carolyn Nichols

Carolyn Nichols
Editor
LOVESWEPT
Bantam Books
666 Fifth Avenue
New York, NY 10103